THE MURDER MAZE

Hugh Fielding, a wealthy advertising man, was killed by an assassin when he opened the door of his rural New England mansion during a violent storm. All of his houseguests were suspect — until it was learned two assassins were hiding outside. Then someone was detected signalling with a flashlight to those killers, which meant someone inside the house was also involved. Police Lieutenant Peter Collier arrived by helicopter, and the investigation got under way . . .

CHARTER
MARK
CUSTOMER SERVICE EXCELLENCE

Kent
County
Council

C153053730

SPECIAL MESSAGE TO READERS

This book is published under the auspices of

THE ULVERSCROFT FOUNDATION

(registered charity No. 264873 UK)

Established in 1972 to provide funds for research, diagnosis and treatment of eye diseases. Examples of contributions made are: —

A Children's Assessment Unit at Moorfield's Hospital, London.

•

Twin operating theatres at the Western Ophthalmic Hospital, London.

•

A Chair of Ophthalmology at the Royal Australian College of Ophthalmologists.

•

The Ulverscroft Children's Eye Unit at the Great Ormond Street Hospital For Sick Children, London.

You can help further the work of the Foundation by making a donation or leaving a legacy. Every contribution, no matter how small, is received with gratitude. Please write for details to:

THE ULVERSCROFT FOUNDATION,
The Green, Bradgate Road, Anstey,
Leicester LE7 7FU, England.
Telephone: (0116) 236 4325

In Australia write to:
THE ULVERSCROFT FOUNDATION,
c/o The Royal Australian College of Ophthalmologists,
27, Commonwealth Street, Sydney,
N.S.W. 2010.

HUNTER LIGGETT

THE MURDER MAZE

Complete and Unabridged

LINFORD
Leicester

First published in Great Britain in 1969 by
Robert Hale Limited
London

First Linford Edition
published 1999
by arrangement with
Robert Hale Limited
London

British Library CIP Data

Liggett, Hunter, *1916*–
The murder maze.—Large print ed.—
Linford mystery library
1. Detective and mystery stories
2. Large type books
I. Title
823.9′14 [F]

ISBN 0–7089–5589–4

Published by
F. A. Thorpe (Publishing) Ltd.
Anstey, Leicestershire

Set by Words & Graphics Ltd.
Anstey, Leicestershire
Printed and bound in Great Britain by
T. J. International Ltd., Padstow, Cornwall

This book is printed on acid-free paper

1

Masters Manor

The night was wild with a lashing rain, with streaks of forked lightning threatening to split heaven and earth asunder, and with a hurrying dark-swollen sky that scarcely cleared the chimney pots.

There were sounds in all directions. The wind tore at eaves, at drain-spouts, at shutters and tree-limbs. It rattled pantiles and slammed an oaken door upon the second floor. It broke its body against the mighty stone façade and screamed in anguish as its spirit departed.

Although Hugh Fielding had said there were these seasonal springtime storms, it seemed improbable that they'd be so fierce and unrelenting. One *did* expect rain-squalls in springtime, even lightning storms and turbulent black skies, but one did not usually anticipate them simultaneously, or, as Mackenzie McAuliffe said, 'This doesn't resemble any spring shower I've ever seen. It's more like the prelude to Judgement Day.'

The grounds were sodden. Across an extensive lawn, ordinarily green and handsome, were the stables, house for domestic staff and a greenhouse. There was also a shed, presumably for maintenance equipment and tools. The only indication of life from that quarter was a miserly trickle of grainy smoke rising from the chimney of the staff quarters.

There was a large riding-ring at the back of the stables, evidently fairly old since the trees that encircled it were enormous things, bending now, whipping and flinging themselves in all directions with the frenzied abandon of the most tortured of rooted living things.

There had once been a kennel adjoining the stables but Hugh Fielding, current owner of Masters Manor, or Masters House as it was called locally, had brought in workmen to demolish the stone structure and remove it because, although Hugh claimed to be fond of dogs, he did not care to breed them, as the former resident of Masters Manor had done — who had been Hugh Fielding's bachelor uncle, Samuel Adams Fielding.

The trees, with rare exceptions, were all old and very large. They were bursting into leaf and this incontinent storm didn't help that condition because new leaves were flying through the air in all directions, or floating helplessly upon some of the water that was everywhere seeking an escape.

None of the people in the house actually feared for the place, although any of them would have admitted that a lightning-strike could indeed shatter a roof or a formidable stone wall. It was, generally speaking, the inconvenience as far as the men were concerned, and the terrifying noise where the women were concerned.

Masters Manor had been through similar storms. For all any one now living knew, it had survived much worse storms. It had been built by Isaiah Grant Fielding in the year of Our Lord 1666, New England's first genuine manor-house-cum-fort. It had withstood numberless Indian assaults, had withstood the French, and in the end, something like a hundred years after erection, had successfully withstood The Rebellion, but in that contention the family had not withstood the rigours of their times as well as the great house had; three sons had gone with the Continentals, their father and his father, then living, plus several nephews, had gone with His Majesty's cause, right on down to the débacle at Yorktown, and afterwards, when the new American nation was harshly disenfranchising Tory natives, taking their homes and businesses, it had been the three sons in the Continental Army who had kept Masters Manor in the Fielding family.

For three hundred years, lacking only an insignificant decade or some such matter, the Fieldings and their stone fort had been identified one with the other. On nights like the present one Hugh's father — dead six years now — had gathered guests around and told them the story of a mad ancestor who'd hanged himself upstairs at the age of forty-five, only moments before the village constable came to arrest him for the murder of a woman in the village. And of course, Hugh's father would never neglect the salient point of that suicide — the corpse was a good three feet off the floor, the rope secured to a beam ten feet distant.

'No mean feat,' he'd say with glittering eyes, 'for a man to haul himself up, then swing back and forth until he could reach a timber ten feet away to tie his own hangrope.'

Invariably someone would ask the inevitable question. Hugh's father would simply smile and point through a rain-streaked window in the direction of the Fielding family cemetery. 'Go see for yourself; it clearly says suicide on his gravestone.'

And so it did. No one ever said, if indeed anyone knew, who had hanged the luckless madman, but as the Manor had *its* legends, so also did the village some mile and a half distant, equally as old, have *its* legends. In this case it was said that when the madman came hastening back to the Manor House, blood on his clothing, screaming gibberish, his own brother and father, realising what he had done, knowing full well the penalty the law would exact, and unwilling to have any such dishonour brought to their name, had hanged the madman themselves.

Hugh, current master, never told that story. He knew it well enough but it had always seemed a bit too melodramatic to be repeated. Hugh was almost a thoroughgoing pragmatist in any case; his advertising business down in New York was very successful. His investments, both local and otherwise, were sound. He had, in fact, achieved a degree of wealth surpassing the similar accomplishments of any of his family up to this time.

He was a modern, handsome, youthful Croesus, and living at Masters Manor was little more to Hugh Fielding than a visit to the countryside; his lavish New York City apartment was much more centrally located to his interests.

The present storm, as far as Hugh was concerned, marked a natural innovation and little else. That he had a houseful of weekend guests, including his only son, Ralph, recently graduated from the university, meant that some of the outdoor entertainment he'd planned would have to be postponed.

He told Emilio Calderon the Central American diplomat-playboy that he was dreadfully sorry things had happened as they had, but he was sure the guests would be able to find indoor amusements, for after all the house, down the years, had been equipped with a billiard room, a splendid dancehall upstairs — complete with gold-leaf stars set in the ceiling — and in one of the cellars there was even a shooting gallery, legacy of Hugh's late father, a genuine, florid-faced country-squire type of person.

Calderon's handsome dark eyes had brightened with sympathy and understanding. He thought the storm would soon pass and the New England summertime sun would then dry things up.

That conversation took place at seven o'clock, shortly after everyone had enjoyed a heavy New England dinner, when the sky should still have been light but was instead as dark as midnight as the eye of the storm came inland to settle directly above the village. Since that time the people at Masters Manor had been preoccupied with the storm.

At nine o'clock, when everyone was sitting in the large living-room having drinks, smoking, struggling to keep a bright and sophisticated conversation alive, the lights failed.

Ralph was able to ascertain by telephone from the village that although there'd been no power failure down there, it was considered very probable a tree had been uprooted somewhere between Brentsboro — the village — and the Manor House, a distance of a mile and a half.

This had happened before, during previous storms. Hugh recalled, as servants brought candles, that his father, annoyed by a similar occurrence years before, had sworn that someday he'd install his own generating plant in one of the cellars. But like many things the previous master had intended doing, this one had never been done either. Hugh's father had been a great sportsman, a hard drinking, thick and powerful man with the voice of a bull and some of the instincts as well — or so local gossip said at any rate.

Frank Olmstead, a wealthy land speculator with world-wide interests, had asked his host to relate the story of the hanged madman. This request was made with a look of sly amusement, and as Olmstead said, the setting was perfect for a ghost story — terrible storm outside, candlelight inside, and a roomful of people who had never heard mention of this sanguine affair. Olmstead had heard of it, he said, on a previous visit to Brentsboro. He was sure the other guests would be intrigued.

Emilio Calderon, a sensitive, quiet, smiling man, wiry and pleasant, murmured reservations. The time was hardly propitious, he thought, if this was a ghost story, and there were several women, wives, present, who probably wouldn't appreciate hearing some tale of anguish, particularly on this night.

Ralph intervened, tactfully suggesting instead that his father relate some of the delightfully amusing stories of Uncle Samuel Adams Fielding, the bachelor brother of Hugh's departed father, who had been master of the manor for a bare eight months after the passing of Hugh's father, and Uncle Samuel Adams Fielding's own demise.

Uncle Samuel had been something of a comic-conservative. Upon one occasion he'd gained notoriety by refusing to pay his income tax because there was a democratic president in the White House. Upon another occasion, trapped by a designing widow in the village, he'd denounced her accusation of betrayal by insisting that, at sixty, although he *had* visited the woman at her cottage, he couldn't possibly have compromised her because she'd thrown him out after only one hour, and as any sane person fully realised, a man of sixty required more time than one hour to strike the proper posture for the variety of intimacy the widow claimed had taken place.

But Frank Olmstead persisted. He told the tale as he'd heard it years before in Brentsboro, which was essentially correct in most respects, but with an unfavourable slant to it as far as the Fieldings were concerned, which of course made it mandatory that Hugh set the record straight.

He stood by the huge fireplace, glass in hand, and told the story in a rather toneless voice. Not especially embarrassed by it — the episode had taken place almost a hundred and fifty years earlier — but not particularly pleased either, for no one, understandably, enjoys admitting that madness had been endemic in a family whose name he bears.

Olmstead, cigar glowing, round, smooth face showing quiet, sardonic amusement, was the only person in the huge living-room with firelight touching them all, who asked no questions after the tale had been told, or who offered no comment. He sat loosely and heavily, smoking and watching his host, his eyes very bright and steady. He seemed almost to relish Hugh's mild discomfort, particularly when someone asked if it had ever been proved that the madman's own kinsmen had hanged him.

Outside, thunder made the mighty house shudder, lightning crackled with a white ferocity, and the downpour never slackened even for a moment. Masters Manor was evidently directly beneath the very centre of the storm. In the candle-light the faces looked pale and tight, until a leap of fireplace flame reddened them, then they didn't look human.

2

The Beginning of a Long Night

Mary-Katherine Plummer had married Frank Olmstead for some reason known only to herself, but it was reasonable to assume Olmstead's wealth hadn't been a very serious deterrent since she'd married him in spite of it although Frank was fifty years old and Mary-Katherine Plummer, three years earlier at the time of the marriage, had been twenty-four, which made her twenty-seven now.

She had large grey eyes, usually wary or hard-looking, a full, sensual mouth, showing early signs of a droop, and the creamy complexion of a schoolgirl. Her hair was red-brown and thick. She was a very striking woman to look at, either standing up or sitting down. She had entertained high hopes of being a great actress and like many spirited women, had found the fact that she lacked acting talent very hard to live with.

She drank a good deal and smoked often. She sat across the Masters Manor living-room watching her husband by candle-light without a trace of any emotion showing. The only time she looked animated at all was when Ralph Fielding suggested billiards. She said she thought it would be fun and left her chair. So did Emilio Calderon, who, a divorced man so rumour said, seemed delighted with the opportunity to escape from the draughty and somehow eerie parlour.

Betty McAuliffe, Mackenzie's lean and juiceless wife, sat beside her curly-haired, handsome and powerfully-built husband watching the others leave the room. Her expression showed no envy at all that Mary-Katherine had two men all to herself. Betty McAuliffe was not a romanticist. She had come to the union with her husband bearing something like two million dollars in dowry. Mackenzie — called Ken by close friends — had married her immediately.

Of course the marriage had been founded upon that wealth, left her by a tobacco-magnate father, and neither Mackenzie nor Betty McAuliffe ever said otherwise. But the odd thing was, they thoroughly liked each other. Ken was a very handsome man, distinguished-looking at forty, outgoing, pleasant, shrewd also, and with an undeniable appeal to women. That no breath of scandal had ever touched his name was remarkable, but perhaps even more remarkable was the way Betty McAuliffe indulgently smiled when younger and prettier women flirted with her husband.

For sophisticated society, the McAuliffe love affair was something people had difficulty in believing. It was just too improbable, but the facts were known: Betty had given every cent of her fortune to her husband, *carte blanche*. He could have thrown her out, in fact, and she admitted she'd have little or no legal recourse.

So it wasn't the money that kept him close to her. It most certainly wasn't her appearance because she was as plain and sexless-looking as a woman could possibly be. That only alternative left for people to believe in, was that Mackenzie McAuliffe loved his wife. A most unique situation; one that even the believers viewed warily, unwilling to relinquish the suspicion that there had to be more to it than just that.

When Betty smiled, as she did when the butler, Dubois, a sturdy, dark French-Canadian brought her fresh ice for the glass in her hand, she looked less plain, but she still didn't look very pretty. She had a nice speaking voice, though. Her 'thank you,' to Dubois was like velvet. The swarthy French-Canadian smiled his appreciation; butler or not, Dubois was a man. That kind of a voice never failed to reach deep down in a man.

It was Betty McAuliffe, when the tale of the hanged madman was concluded, who tried to brighten the mood by recalling what Ralph Fielding had said about Uncle Samuel Adams Fielding.

Hugh responded with a smile in her direction, told the tale of Uncle Sam's near-thing with the amorous widow, and got laughter from everyone but Frank Olmstead, who smiled and smoked his cigar and kept watching Hugh Fielding with the eyes of a confident shark.

The thunder, still intermittently shaking Masters Manor, eventually seemed to be receding. The lightning however, still struck with jagged streaks in all directions. It seemed incredible that the great old stone house could continue to escape, but it did.

The rain did not lessen, but except for the mess it made of the riding-ring, the grounds, the cowed countryside, it offered no genuine threat. The area around the manor house was well drained.

In fact, as the night advanced, it was the rainfall which seemed to have a soporific effect. Betty McAuliffe yawned discreetly behind a useless scrap of lace in her hand, a large, square-cut diamond on her wedding-ring finger catching and hurling back the red-orange light of the log fire.

Frank Olmstead finished his drink and his cigar but made no move to rise. Instead he asked Hugh how his uncle had come out when he'd defied the government over income tax.

Hugh answered whimsically, a mood the recollection of his uncle usually brought forth in him. 'He paid. The Bureau of Internal Revenue sent around several agents. Uncle Sam frightened the first two off. He was a powerfully built man even in his late years, and gave the impression of being a regular gladiator. Then the bureau sent a woman agent.' Hugh smiled into Frank's eyes. 'Uncle Sam paid, penalty, interest and all, but he went down with all flags flying, denouncing the President, the Congress, the liberal wing of both political parties, and the Commissioner of Inland Revenue. He had the woman agent to lunch, took her on a tour of the estate, then wrote her out a cheque for the full amount.'

'Interesting,' murmured Olmstead. 'A very interesting family, in fact. Different, but interesting.'

Mary-Katherine returned to the room followed by Emilio Calderon and Ralph Fielding. The men were holding candlesticks aloft. All three of them were in a pleasant mood, but moments later when Frank gave his wife a long, unsmiling look, she sank into the chair she'd vacated earlier with that same disillusioned, somewhat sulky expression.

The telephone rang in the study. Dubois appeared at the door to say Mister Fielding Senior was wanted. Hugh departed and Frank Olmstead turned to face Ralph.

'Your father just told us some anecdotes about Uncle Sam. What are your recollections of him, Ralph?'

The younger man gazed thoughtfully at Olmstead. There was very little liking in that glance. 'He was a gruff, tough old unreconstructed conservative. He believed in the old-time virtues, Mister Olmstead, but if you think he was some kind of comic, you're wrong.'

There was no mistaking the look that passed between the younger, and older, man. Ralph did not like Frank Olmstead, and there was reason to believe this sentiment was mutual.

Olmstead said, 'How about your grandfather — your father's father; was he a typical Fielding as well?'

Ralph's tanned, rather squarely handsome face tightened noticeably, even by candle-light. 'Typical Fielding?' he purred. 'Meaning what, Mister Olmstead?'

Evidently the older man across the room heard menace in the voice if he failed to detect it in the shadowy face, because, with an expansive gesture, Olmstead said, 'Nothing in particular, Ralph. Only one of your predecessors hanged his own son; another refused to pay his taxes because he didn't like the President. Your father's father must have had eccentricities as well. That's all I meant. An interesting family . . .' Olmstead heaved to his feet and, smiling at Ralph, crossed to his wife's chair and held out his hand. 'I think it's time for bed anyway.'

They all murmured something polite as the Olmsteads took one of the candle-holders and headed for the wide staircase with its oak banister. Ralph watched them go up the steps with that same thoughtful expression on his face, as though he were speculating about something that interested him.

Mackenzie McAuliffe and his wife were the next pair to bid the others goodnight and go hiking up the dark stairway. Only Ralph and Emilio Calderon were left when Hugh returned from the study to announce that his caller had been one of the men who supervised the electric company's sub-station down in Brentsboro. A crew had been dispatched to locate the break in the power line, and with any luck at all by morning electricity should be restored.

Emilio said he liked candle-light. He laughed. 'But of course when it is to be shared only by men, it somehow loses its charm.'

Hugh smiled. He'd met Calderon at an Alliance For Progress bazaar sponsored the previous year by the Organisation of American States, and had liked him — as nearly everyone invariably did — right from the start. Emilio was good company. He was reputed to be wealthy but no one seemed to know much about him beyond the obvious fact that he dressed expensively and drove a beautiful Jaguar car.

Ralph told his father the others had retired. He then said, 'Who is Frank Olmstead? I know, you told me he was some kind of business associate, but beyond that — who is he?'

Hugh eyed his son blankly. 'Beyond that . . . ? I don't know, exactly. He is a speculator. Mostly, he deals in land, in leases, in oil and port facilities. But what else he might be I have no idea, except that it seems to me those things ought to keep him busy enough.'

'He seems to want an awful lot of information about the family, Dad.'

Hugh shrugged and examined the highball glass he put aside to answer the telephone. It was still half full, although that was probably due to melting ice. 'Just talk, Ralph; just casual interest to help pass an otherwise frustrating evening.' Hugh sank into a large, dark leather chair and hoisted his glass, eyeing his son over the rim quizzically. 'Olmstead's business requires memorising many seemingly unrelated bits of information.'

'About us?' asked Ralph.

'No. But it's his nature to ask

questions, to make assessments.'

Ralph looked at Emilio, who was seeking a speck of something on his coat-front, evidently slightly embarrassed to be sitting there, a third member to what was more or less a family conversation. Emilio did not look up.

Ralph said, 'I guess it was just my imagination. Anyway it's late.' He arose smiling. 'Goodnight, you two.'

Hugh and Emilio smiled. They were silent until the soft footfalls going up the stairway were lost, then Hugh said, 'There's a lot of his mother in Ralph. She had a tough nature, Emilio.'

Calderon was baffled. 'Tough . . . ?'

'Well: she wondered about people a lot; about their motives, their personalities, their convictions.'

Emilio thought on that. 'Unusual in a woman, it seems to me.'

Hugh agreed. 'She was an unusual woman. We'd have had more children, but she was killed in an aircraft accident.' Hugh drained the tepid drink and put the glass aside. 'Seven years ago.'

Emilio was properly contrite. 'I'm very

sorry. Still; isn't seven years a long time?'

Hugh smiled softly. 'You see, I think where we differ most, Emilio, is that you are a romanticist. I'm not. I'm like the old dog whose habits can't be broken. Every time I've met another woman . . . ' Hugh heaved his wide shoulders up, then down ' . . . it would never work for me.'

'I see. A one-woman man. I don't think I've ever known one before.'

Hugh said, 'Sure you have. Take almost any man my age — fifty this past summer — and if you dig down you'll find he's not very willing to give up his independence or his memories just for having his meals on time, or being dragged round to the charity dances and first nights at the theatres.'

'Well; then it isn't altogether fidelity, is it? It is the sinking down without a struggle into dull habits.'

Hugh laughed. 'Maybe that's it. What do you say we get some sleep? Perhaps by morning the electricity will be restored, and the sun will be shining. I thought of taking everyone on a tour of the area. I'm sure you'd find it pleasant — in a dull sort of way.'

They smiled, rose, and headed for the stairs, one behind the other. Dubois appeared, hovering in a doorway as Hugh came forward. He asked in a low, throaty voice whether it would be correct for him to now close and lock the downstairs. Hugh nodded and plodded ahead. Emilio was already halfway up the stairs, candle in hand, casting a grotesque, crouched shadow upon the tapestried wall.

The rain still fell, undiminished, but there was no more thunder and only an occasional flash of white-hot brilliance. The storm seemed to be moving out of the area.

3

Disaster!

To be rich and successful is a never-ending source of private gratification, but Hugh lay in his bed gazing into the pitchblende blackness feeling numb about so many things.

Wealth had surrounded him all his life, and comfort too, then he had compounded it by proving to be gifted in the accumulation of more wealth, which had to be some kind of psychological slip-up since he'd never actually possessed any sense of urgency in that direction.

He was artistic. It was hard to look at him and say this was so, for he looked every inch a patrician man's-man, and he was. He'd survived a war — with decorations. He'd travelled the world without anyone's assistance. He'd won a much sought-after bride, and he'd proved himself mature with superior logic a hundred times, but as he lay now thinking of many things and deriving little if any satisfaction from them, he thought of himself as a man who had let life slip by.

He'd had these same thoughts several months earlier, not long after his fiftieth birthday. There were no longer any distant trumpets nor any high-aloft grand banners. Money was handy, money was taken, money was accumulated, and it remained nothing but money.

Ralph was a source of pride. He'd go to Law School in the autumn.

But what else was left over from yesterday except a crushed rose in a book in his study, or the silver-framed picture of a level-eyed, handsome woman, a little too serious perhaps, but loving.

A lot of kaleidoscopic, disconnected, pointless memories. Youth was gone like a boy laughing as he ran down a sunlighted path, out of sight forever. Love was gone. Money remained. Prestige, position, success, the thriving ad agency in New York City, the sophisticated apartment, the deference of doormen, lift–operators, secretaries, clerks, associates.

'Jesus,' he whispered in the darkness, hurled back the covers, rose and went to stand by the closed, streaked window. There was a foreboding, a chill round his heart. Money was piling up all around him; he imagined himself suffocating in the stuff, drowning in it while someone whose face he couldn't distinguish, stood aside and roared with laughter.

Then there was an odd pinprick of light. His whole attention closed down upon that until it dawned upon him it wasn't part of the brooding mood, it was a real light down below in the area at the front of the house. It seemed to be following the curve of the long drive from roadway to house but with the water standing everywhere he couldn't be certain.

The light halted, swung left, swung right, picked up the dun millrace on ahead, and began moving again. It was most certainly being carried by someone out in the downpour but Hugh could not make out any human shape.

Obviously, though, there was nothing sinister going on, otherwise surely whoever that was down there wouldn't be struggling through the storm towards the front door with a lighted torch.

Still and all . . . Hugh flung off his robe, dressed hurriedly, took the loaded automatic from his bedside table, checked the clip to be sure, then rummaged in a dark closet for a heavy waterproof jacket which effectively hid the gun as well as it also promised protection from the damp chill of late night.

He reached the landing, saw only the faintest shine from coals in the fireplace, tried a light-switch without any luck, and started down the stairs. He'd got halfway along when he heard a sound and looked back. Ralph was up there leaning on the railing. 'What's going on?' he called quietly. 'Did you see someone outside with a light?'

Hugh confirmed this and said, 'Go on back to bed. Probably someone whose car stalled in the water. I'll bring him in and get him settled for the night.' He resumed his way, reached the ground-level and went directly to the front door. Ralph may have still been up there, it was too darkly distant to make sure of that.

The rain was coming straight down now, veritable sheets of cold water. Fortunately the door was recessed; stood back some six or eight feet with a massive stone entry on both sides, and with an oaken-beamed porch overhead. When Hugh opened the door cold air hit him, damp and unpleasant, but no actual rain came in.

The only thing he afterwards remembered was the blinding flash of light and the sound of an explosion, although in recollection the sound seemed distant while the blinding brilliance had been very close to his face.

He had no recollection of being hurled back into the house, or of falling, or of hearing voices suddenly raised from a number of different directions. All he was conscious of for a moment or two, was the delicious sense of increasing warmth and looseness that came up from inside him somewhere in successive waves, each one darker than the former one.

Ralph reached him first. He called loudly and rolled Hugh on to his back. Then he let off a cry for assistance, again and again. Meanwhile, the door stood open, the cold air came in, and it wasn't possible to see ten feet out into the grey, drowning world beyond where that light had been.

Dubois didn't arrive. He was blissfully sleeping in the distant staff quarters which, although actually only a couple of hundred yards distant, might as well have been several miles off because the noise of the deluge blotted out all other sounds. No one thought to ring Dubois on the telephone, everyone was too concerned for Hugh.

The men carried him into the study where there was a large sofa. There, placing blankets beneath him to keep things tidy, they arranged him in the most comfortable position.

Frank Olmstead cursed because they had no electricity and the candles, brought hastily, were not sufficient. 'But I'll tell you this much,' Olmstead said savagely. 'Someone sure as hell shot him. You see that puffed-up jagged-looking hole? That, my friends, wasn't made by any streak of lightning.'

He made that last statement in sarcastic reference to Ralph having mentioned seeing a bright light, like lightning, seconds before he saw his father go backwards in a violent fall.

'And that sound wasn't thunder, my friends. That was a gunshot. Don't tell me different because I've heard too many of them in my lifetime. Why can't we have some gawddamned *light* in here?'

Emilio took Ralph aside. 'Telephone for a physician,' he urged. 'Do so at once. That is a serious wound, I can tell even from this distance.'

Ralph left the room. There was a telephone on the desk but he either forgot it was there or chose not to use it in front of all the people crowding around the couch where his father lay as pale as death in the flickering light of six or eight candles.

Mackenzie McAuliffe left his wife's side — she hadn't had time to dress and stood by the door angular and stone-like — to get closer to the sofa and kneel. Frank Olmstead stepped away, went to a decanter on a dark-oak sideboard and poured himself a great slug of red wine. It wasn't suitable for his needs but there was nothing else.

He turned looking at them all, his heavy round face ugly and slit-eyed. 'He must have heard them knocking or something; must have recognised them — maybe.' He turned to re-fill his glass. When he turned back again Ralph was behind Betty McAuliffe looking towards the couch. Olmstead said, 'Did anyone hear the bell ring? How else did he know there was someone down here?'

Ralph explained about the electric torch; he'd seen it too. He told of meeting his father on the way down and what Hugh had said. 'Something about a wayfarer stranded by the storm. He said he'd put him in one of the guest bedrooms for the night.'

'Wait a minute,' exclaimed Olmstead, holding his re-filled glass and scowling. 'Are you saying your father didn't *know* who was at the door?'

Ralph moved silently closer to the sofa where Mackenzie McAuliffe was doing something to the body lying there, by the light Emilio was holding for him. Ralph didn't answer so Olmstead said, 'That could have been *any of us* then, opening that damned door.'

Betty McAuliffe said, 'Hardly, Mister Olmstead; I don't open doors in houses where I'm a houseguest. That's up to the master and mistress.'

Olmstead gazed steadily at Betty, who returned his look without blinking. He dropped his glance, finally, to the glass he was holding. 'All right, maybe that's it. He came to the door knowing Fielding would answer it. And he shot him.'

Emilio leaned and said something in an urgent whisper. McAuliffe nodded, raised his face and said, 'Ralph, when'll the doctor get here?'

'He isn't in the village,' Ralph replied. 'He was called out more than two hours earlier to care for a woman who had a heart attack at one of the farms.'

McAuliffe digested this and came right

back. 'Which farm? We've got to find him, Ralph. We've got to get him here as soon as we possibly can even if one of us has to drive down there and drag him away.'

Mary-Katherine bent over the back of the sofa, looked, then hastily turned and went to a little chair in a gloomy corner and sat down.

Emilio straightened a little, holding his candle higher. 'Does anyone know how to tie off blood vessels?'

No one answered.

Olmstead downed his wine and put the glass from him, went over where his wife huddled and patted her shoulder with a noticeable awkwardness.

Betty McAuliffe went forward, lean and shapeless and with her plain features set in a hard expression. She touched her husband's back gently. 'Do it, Ken,' she said evenly. 'Improvise but do it. Do *something*. Emilio; give me that candle and get several more. It's too dark here.'

Everyone moved at once, as though the shock had passed for each of them at the identical moment. They got candles. Frank Olmstead left the room and returned moments later with a fistful of the things, which he proceeded to light and pass around until there was a fairly bright, soft light over and around the sofa.

Betty touched her husband again. They looked at one another then Mackenzie leaned closer and went to work. The only sound was of pouring rain. Even the lightning had finally deserted them.

The telephone rang. Everyone jumped. Ralph stepped away and grabbed up the instrument. It was the supervisor for the electric company calling to say his crew had called in on their wireless to report that they'd found the broken line, and as had been suspected, an uprooted tree had broken it. He said the repairs would be completed within an hour and hoped there hadn't been too much inconvenience. Ralph thanked the man, rang off, then lifted the telephone again and dialled the office of the State Police down at Brentsboro. The telephone rang twice then no more.

Ralph looked at the instrument he was holding, broke that connection and dialled again. This time he got no responsive sound at all. The telephone had succumbed exactly as the electricity had.

Mary-Katherine and her husband were staring at the telephone in Ralph's hand. He put the thing back upon its cradle and stood for a moment without moving. The only sound anyone made was a little half-sigh, half-moan from Mackenzie McAuliffe who was kneeling beside the sofa.

It was a macabre scene, six people in various stages of undress, gathered round a sofa where a limp, grey-faced man lay drenched with blood, holding aloft candles and scarcely seeming to breathe.

A fresh wind rose, out of the north, and rattled the roof as it passed over hurrying southward. When it diminished it seemed that the rain was also slackening off somewhat. At least instead of the constant drumming there were intermittent moments of gusty pounding, then the steady descent again. The storm might have been passing, at last. There'd been no thunder, no lightning, and except for that vagrant high wind, no real blow for some time now. But the ghostly gathering in Hugh Fielding's black-oak-panelled study seemed not to notice.

McAuliffe eventually stopped whatever he was doing, knelt stiffly for a moment, then slowly and almost with practised grace rested his curly head upon his outstretched arms.

Betty, bending over from the rear, laid a cool, gentle hand upon her husband's neck and kept it there.

4

Three Men Left

Ralph, feeling correctly that his place was at his father's side, asked Emilio or Olmstead or one of the others to make the hazardous drive to Brentsboro and send back the police, then continue on and find the physician.

Mackenzie McAuliffe rose and wiped scarlet hands upon a towel his wife held forth, presumably rustled from the kitchen.

'There's no need,' he said. 'Hugh is dead.'

Only Ralph moved, the others stood like statues while Hugh's son went to drop down on one knee. Mackenzie had pulled a robe someone had brought up to Hugh's chin, decently concealing the gaping, wet, red hole in his body. Hugh seemed to be pleasantly sleeping. His expression was relaxed, almost smiling. There was the tell-tale greyness of someone depleted of blood but there was also that tinted candle-light that concealed details.

Emilio Calderon went to lift the telephone and listen for dialling tone. He put the instrument down gently, looking disappointed. A moment later he caught the eyes of McAuliffe and Olmstead, jerked his head and glided silently from the room with the other men following.

Beyond earshot, in the great living-room, near the fireplace because there was a definite clamminess to the house now, Emilio said, 'Someone will have to try and reach the village. The telephone is still out of order. Gentlemen; Hugh was murdered. Unless the police are alerted right away perhaps the murderer will escape.'

'Or,' growled Olmstead with a scowl, 'kill someone else. One of us, maybe.'

McAuliffe looked long at the older, larger man, before he said, 'Are you implying there's someone out there in this storm who is mad — who goes about shooting people out of hand?'

'Fielding's dead isn't he?' shot back Olmstead, glowering.

'He may have had a dangerous personal enemy,' exclaimed McAuliffe. 'It seems slightly far-fetched to me, to say there's a maniac out there.'

'Those things happen,' retorted Olmstead stoutly.

'Pick up any newspaper; there are armed nuts wandering around shooting people for no apparent reason every day.' Olmstead thought a second then added: 'Even in storms like this one.'

Emilio, seeing the purpose for which he'd got these men together, getting lost in some kind of minor dispute, broke in and said, 'Please, whether he's still out there waiting to shoot another of us, or whether he was Hugh's private enemy, we still must get the police very quickly.'

McAuliffe nodded at Calderon, 'I'll go.'

From the doorway a pleasant voice said, 'No you won't go; let one of the servants attempt it, or some single person.' Betty McAuliffe was standing there holding her plain terry-cloth robe tight to her flat, angular body. The three men turned to gaze at her. She only saw one of them — her husband.

'Hugh is dead,' she explained in that same very calm, soothing voice. 'If, as Mister Olmstead says, that killer is out there in the night, he can't get another victim unless one of us goes out there to him, can he?'

'How do we summon help?' asked Calderon. 'The telephone does not work at all.'

'Wait,' said Betty, hugging herself against the clammy chill. 'Wait at least for daylight. By then the lights will be on again. Also by then, perhaps the telephone company will have that instrument functioning again. But it just isn't reasonable for one of us to walk out to the cars in this storm, and try to reach Brentsboro only to tell someone Hugh Fielding has been murdered. Even granting that the cars will not be drowned out, after all, they've been sitting out through the entire storm, and even granting that the roads aren't washed out and that one could reach the village.'

Neither Olmstead nor Emilio Calderon argued, but Mackenzie said, 'Betty, if he *is* out there, and if he *is* some kind of compulsive killer, don't kid yourself, love, if we don't go to him he'll come to us.'

'There are guns in the house, Ken. Ralph told me that.'

Her husband nodded, regarding the angular woman with a tender glance. 'We'd need an army to establish siege-positions, in a house as large as this, Betty. And very probably *he* is familiar with the grounds as well as the house. Otherwise, how did he come directly to the front door as Ralph said he did, and . . . '

'All houses have front doors, Ken. He followed the driveway.'

'And knew his victim would answer the door, Betty?'

'Well, it was a safe assumption, wasn't it? Normally, the master of the house opens the door at that hour of the night, with the servants gone to quarters.'

Ken nodded. 'You're forgetting one thing, darling. This killer knew his victim.'

She could dispute that easily, and she did so. 'He knew *a* victim, Ken. As Mister Olmstead said earlier — suppose one of the others of us had opened that door?'

'Please,' interrupted Emilio again. 'Mrs. McAuliffe, your husband will stay and I will go.'

Three faces turned to regard the wiry, dark-eyed Central-American. Wind-driven rain struck against a nearby leaded window with the sound of ten dozen elfin fists. Although the downpour seemed to have diminished somewhat, now there was a fresh wind disturbed the raw and pitch-black night. The only thing one could see beyond that window was streaked, criss-crossing patches of water. Otherwise there was no depth to the night; it was as though the world had shrunk so small that only Masters Manor still existed and everything else had been swept away or inundated beneath an ebon tide.

'You should have a gun,' said Betty to Emilio Calderon, sounding like a mother saying, very practically, her child should put on a jacket if he was going out into the cold. 'I'll go and get one from Ralph.' She departed, still clutching the uninspiring terry-cloth robe to her uninspiring body.

Olmstead lit a cigar, ran a hand through his thin, stringy hair, looked at Emilio then turned to regard the watery window. 'Maybe she's right,' he muttered. 'Fielding *is* dead. No doctor's going to reverse that. And if we wait for daylight . . . ' Olmstead didn't finish, he blew a fragrant cloud into the chill and backed closer to the sullen coals upon the hearthstone.

Mackenzie stared fixedly at the window lost in private speculation. Emilio left them to get a coat from his upstairs bedroom. Climbing the dark stairs he looked even thinner, more wiry, than he actually was. The wind rose making an unpleasant scratching sound under the high eaves and Frank Olmstead turned towards McAuliffe.

'It didn't have to be some maniac out there, you know, McAuliffe. It could have been someone from *inside* the house.'

Mackenzie's brooding eyes considered his companion a moment. 'What are you talking about?' he demanded. 'You saw what happened when Ralph yelled for help. Within moments we were all down here — dry. If one of us had been outside he'd have got drenched.'

'Not with the proper foul-weather gear, he wouldn't have.'

Mackenzie's face darkened with annoyance. 'This is ridiculous, Olmstead.'

'Why is it?'

'I just told you. Even wearing oilskins, if one of us had been out there, had shot Fielding, he wouldn't have been able to get inside, shed the rain-clothes and still reach Ralph and his father when all the others also reached him.'

'Sure he could have,' said Olmstead quietly. 'Because he didn't turn after shooting Hugh and run back, McAuliffe; he didn't run away at all.'

'No?'

'No. He waited in the darkness out of

sight until Ralph was down on his knees beside Hugh, his back to the front door, and he stepped *inside*, stepped around towards any of the dark corners, shed his oilskins and when everyone was excited and confused, all he had to do was grab a candle and join in.'

Mackenzie stood gazing at Frank Olmstead as though he thought the man were making a very poor joke. He didn't even offer a rebuttal although one certainly occurred to him: If Olmstead were correct, then somewhere in this very room there should be a crumpled set of oilskins. Or, if in the ensuing confusion the killer had managed to conceal them, there should still be a puddle of water where they'd been. There was no way to make the water disappear.

Emilio returned walking lightly forward on the balls of his feet. He was wearing a tweed coat and a somewhat shapeless felt hat with a ridiculously narrow brim, scarcely the kind of attire to challenge a storm in.

Betty also returned, with a flat, ugly automatic pistol in her left hand, the weight of the thing dragging her wrist downward. Emilio smiled, his white teeth showing gaily in the gloom as he took the gun and thanked Betty for it, almost as though it had been a spray of flowers.

They stood a moment in strained silence. Emilio pushed the automatic into his waistband, still smiling. 'I feel like something out of a bad television picture,' he said.

Ralph appeared in the doorway of his father's study, eyes dull with shock but perfectly rational. He stared at Calderon. 'What are you doing?' he demanded. 'Emilio, you can't go out there.'

Calderon opened the tweed coat to disclose the pistol against his flat stomach. He shrugged in a purely Latin response, indicating without using words that he was as well prepared to make the effort as anyone else, including anyone who might be waiting out in the darkness.

Ralph crossed over to the little group in front of the fireplace. 'Forget it,' he said, a little harshly. 'It's got to be a deranged person. The wisest thing for all of us is to remain inside, keep all doors and windows locked, and wait for dawn. If one of us has to try to reach the village by then, at least the others can watch from the windows and perhaps protect him that way.'

'Sound,' murmured Olmstead, chewing his cigar. 'Sound thinking.'

McAuliffe stared at him. Olmstead seemed to possess a chameleon-like capacity for going from one viewpoint to another without a second thought or even an apology to himself. Up until this moment he'd favoured Calderon's departure; now he no longer did. The man was a genuine enigma.

Betty McAuliffe drifted up behind Ralph Fielding like a thin ghost. She stood back there still clutching her robe, looking and listening.

Emilio, whose original idea it had been to try and reach Brentsboro, would not relinquish his proposal so readily. 'Listen to me,' he said, addressing Ralph. 'If it is an insane person out there, he is not going to let things remain as they are until daylight. If he is homicidal, Ralph, he is going to try again, and again.

Staying in the house like frightened rats won't help.' Emilio made a wide gesture with both arms. 'Your father showed me through this house yesterday. It is a sieve, my friend. You can lock all the doors and windows and I promise you, if I were outside and wanted to be inside, there are a dozen ways I could manage it, locked doors and windows notwithstanding.'

Olmstead began nodding his head. No one paid him much attention. Betty, studying Calderon, seemed suddenly to shudder and gather the terry-cloth robe tighter. She lifted her head and looked over where those dark-shadowed stairs led to the upper floor. Calderon's logic had evidently struck her as sound. Then she turned and slowly retraced her steps back into the candle-lit study where Hugh Fielding lay.

Calderon moved forward, laid a hand upon Ralph's arm and smiled gently. 'You see? And there is something more: Your father deserves better from his friends than to lie in there while we whimper like cowards, afraid to see that he is avenged.' The long fingers closed down like steel, then dropped off Ralph's arm. Calderon crossed the room to the large, oak front door and never hesitated. Pulling the door open, admitting a cold blast of wet wind, he stepped through and hauled the door closed after himself.

At once Mackenzie McAuliffe came to life. 'Get to the windows,' he said, and made the first move, although it was too dark out to be able to watch Calderon's progress, and even if any of them had actually seen Calderon attacked out there, they had no weapons to succour him with.

Still, Olmstead and Ralph Fielding blindly obeyed, moving towards the windows along the front of the house. They saw nothing and except for the wailing of the high wind, heard nothing.

Betty returned, stood in the centre of the room and said, 'Did he really go out there?'

None of the men answered her as they strained to see beyond the streaked glass into the wild night beyond.

5

Calderon's Strange Return

Mary-Katherine Olmstead did not want to stay in the dark study where the corpse lay, understandably, and in fact when she sought her husband she tarried at his side only momentarily, then drifted towards the far end of the huge living-room where the bar was discreetly placed, to mix herself a drink. Two drinks.

Above the bar on a back-wall was an old oil painting of a square-jawed Fielding with mutton-chop whiskers down both his leathery cheeks. He had hard little blue eyes and an uncompromising wound for a mouth. Whether he'd been hung there after the bar had been built, or whether he'd already been hanging there before, the effect was the same. He dampened the spirits, drinking and otherwise, of his beholders sitting at the bar.

Eventually, all the surviving people in

Masters Manor gravitated around Mary-Katherine, and Ralph stepped around behind the bar to make drinks, stonily unresponsive to the little that was said among his father's — now his — houseguests. When he'd finished setting up filled glasses he suggested that Olmstead and McAuliffe accompany him on a tour of the house to make certain all windows were locked, all doors bolted. The men were agreeable but stood a moment nursing their drinks and listening to the gritting sound of rain slashing obliquely against windowpanes.

Mary-Katherine raised a hand to brush back dark-copper hair and speak — and at that precise instant the lights came on. Whatever it was Mary-Katherine was going to say, she, like the others, was so surprised at the house being filled with cheerful light, she didn't say it.

McAuliffe twisted on his bar-stool to gaze towards the study. The lights were on in there too. He said, 'With luck the telephone will also function,' and slid off the stool to take his drink with him and walk over to ascertain whether this was true or not.

None of them said anything until Ralph Fielding reminded Frank Olmstead that they hadn't gone round making certain the house was securely locked from the inside. Frank only shrugged, watching the study doorway with a close and narrow intentness.

Mackenzie McAuliffe appeared in the doorway shaking his head. The telephone still did not function. Betty watched her husband coming back across the room and said, 'If they've fixed the electrical circuits they may also look after the telephone shortly.'

Perhaps the fact that the electric company and telephone company were separate entities had escaped Betty McAuliffe, or perhaps she had the common-enough great faith in large public service industries. Whatever it was the way she said those words had a very soothing effect upon the others. So much so, in fact, that although the telephone was not operable, Frank Olmstead said it was too bad Calderon had already gone, because if he'd only stayed in the house a while longer there'd probably have been no need for his departure.

Ralph came from behind the bar bringing to the attention of the two other men that matter of the locked doors and windows. The three of them started away leaving Betty McAuliffe and Mary-Katherine Olmstead alone at the bar. Betty had a very practical thought: It was cold and clammy in the living-room, yet there was a large, recessed woodbox beside the fireplace which was amply stocked, so she suggested that Mary-Katherine lend her a hand at getting a decent blaze going. Mary-Katherine was perfectly agreeable. The amount of liquor she'd drunk over the past fifteen or twenty minutes hadn't really been such a terrible amount, but Mary-Katherine couldn't handle much liquor, and she'd drunk fast. Those things made the difference; she went to help Betty with a flourish and a flounce.

Upstairs the men separated in the long hallway, two of them, Mackenzie and Frank Olmstead, splitting off on each side to examine windows along the east and west sides of the house. Ralph went ahead of them to a little dead-end annexe that wasn't more than six or eight feet deep and which bisected the main hallway. At the end of this passageway was a heavy metal door, obviously installed several hundred years after Masters Manor had been erected.

Ralph reached with the gesture of a man knowing exactly what he'd find, gave the handle a twist and push, then turned back at once because the door had refused to yield. Beyond it was a spidery metal ladderwork down across the rear of the house — a fire-escape.

He waited at the south end of the hallway for Frank and Mackenzie to complete their inspection. He lit a cigarette, leaned upon the wall gazing directly towards the distant staircase leading down to the first floor, and seemed engrossed. In several ways he resembled his father; he was a tallish man, handsome in a square-jawed, rugged way, and possessed that kind of poise only very secure and very confident people ever possess.

A great wave of wind struck the north end of the house making the entire structure shudder. Olmstead came out of an empty guestroom, shook his head wryly at Ralph then went into the next room.

When the three of them stood together, finally, Ralph said he hadn't really expected any doors or windows up there to be open, and led off for the first-floor. By this time the men, excepting Ralph, were able to feel some degree of returning confidence. Doubtless the wonderful brightness of electric light contributed considerably to that mood.

The front of the house was locked, all but the main door through which Emilio had passed. Ralph locked it.

They spoke briefly with the women, who had a splendid blaze going, then trooped off to inspect the kitchen-area. Here, there was an outside door in almost every room, even including a Dutch-door, half-wood, half-glass between the extensive rear gardens and a sunroom that

Ralph explained had been his mother's sewing-room, then his father, after her passing, had had the entire west wall glassed-in.

But the doors were locked. Mackenzie recalled the butler saying something about locking up, or thought he had at any rate, and Ralph nodded his head. It was Dubois's final obligation each night.

Ralph took them back through the huge, glistening kitchen to a little butler's pantry where a narrow little old door squeezed over against the stone wall gave way to a stone stairway leading into what appeared to be the dark bowels of the earth. There was an unhealthy, mouldy smell that came up to the three men, chilly and damp. Without a word Ralph flicked a switch just inside the door and started down, each footfall echoing eerily in the regions below. None of them had an electric torch, but as long as there were lights in this dungeon-like place no torch was needed.

The cellar, Ralph explained, had been enlarged after the house had been built. The main vault, where they stood while he related all this, had been excavated first, for a storehouse, a purpose it still served as one could see by the cupboards and shelves on all four walls. But across this room, which was perhaps twenty by twenty, there was an arched stone opening, doorless, and a passageway. Ralph took them over there, ducked to pass through the none-too-high opening, and his footsteps at once were muffled by packed earth. In the main vault there'd been a fieldstone floor, perhaps to discourage dampness in New England's long winters from seeping upwards out of the ground, but in this other section of the cellar the floor was simply iron-like packed earth.

Here too, were another pair of rooms, one just as large as the main vault, the other one smaller, cement-walled, and white washed. This room held the powerful oil-burning furnace that, with the help of a large blowing unit, kept Masters Manor warm in winter, and air-conditioned in summer.

From this room, over towards the west wall, there was an earthen ramp instead of stairs, leading upwards towards a pair of storm-doors. These were hinged on opposite sides and slanted heavily as though from the outside they'd appear almost flush with the surrounding grounds. That other room, across the dungeon-passageway from this furnace-room, according to Ralph Fielding, was a sort of storeroom for broken furniture and the like, and had no door at all and no window. He said his grandfather had made beer and ale in that room many decades ago, and the smell was still discernible.

As Ralph was explaining about these nether regions he was walking up the earthen ramp towards the storm-doors. Both Olmstead and McAuliffe saw him slip, catch his balance and stop to look steadily at something at his feet a moment before moving on up to the doors. Ralph's narrative ended in mid-sentence while he reached to test the doors.

It was never resumed. The storm-doors were not only unlocked, but what Ralph had slipped in, glaringly clear in the brightness of the room, was water. Not water that had leaked through past the storm-doors because there was no telltale rivulet, but water that lay in a small puddle, and as each man turned slowly to follow those puddles they went downward from the ramp until, fading out near the furnace-room doorway, became lost.

'Footprints,' said Mackenzie crisply, pointing to the intervals, to the gradually emerging outline. 'Footprints of someone who came through those doors out of the rain. Would it be one of the servants, Ralph?'

It was an almost pointless question since the water was comparatively fresh and the servants had retired many hours earlier. Ralph shook his head.

Olmstead and McAuliffe studied the damp outlines while Ralph raised one of the storm-doors, which were massive wooden things heavily creosoted to prevent rotting, and poked his head out into the wind-whipped rain. But there was nothing to be seen; it was so dark out there a man, or even a company of men, could have been standing twenty feet away and Ralph wouldn't have been able to make them out.

He closed the door, twisted the lock, tried both doors to make sure he'd locked them, then pulled out a handkerchief to mop rainwater off his face and neck.

McAuliffe stepped to the door of the furnace-room and peered across into the doorless room opposite, the place where eternal night lay in deep layers of the room Ralph had said was only a store-room. Olmstead joined him, but neither of them went any closer until Ralph, putting up his damp handkerchief, pressed past into the passageway, lit by a single naked bulb midway, and stepped over into the storeroom's opening. If any of those damp footprints were in this other room they were not discernible.

Olmstead said, 'Turn on the light, Ralph. There is one isn't there?'

Ralph answered without looking around. 'No. Not in here.'

Olmstead muttered something under his breath as McAuliffe stepped across the passageway to peer into the store-room. He raised a cigarette lighter but Olmstead, behind him, said, 'Don't outline us, McAuliffe. If he's in there he's armed.'

The words sounded hollow in the timeless hush of this musty place where even the storm couldn't penetrate with its sounds.

Ralph Fielding stepped all the way into the room and began to turn very slowly, peering into the darkness where stacked old chairs, dust-laden tables, even some paintings, were stacked or hung in haphazard fashion. He drew in his breath sharply and froze in his tracks. The men behind him, alerted to something amiss, became instantly motionless.

Ralph bent slightly from the waist, staring hard, then he moved suddenly and swiftly to the left of the doorway and said, '*Emilio!*'

McAuliffe finally depressed the trigger of his lighter. Olmstead, staring over McAuliffe's shoulder, made an explosive oath.

Emilio Calderon was lying, limp and soggy, upon his face over beside the east wall. McAuliffe's feeble light showed little more than the body's flat outline until

Ralph summoned McAuliffe closer. Ralph knelt and very gently rolled Calderon over on to his back.

The little pencil-thin flame that McAuliffe lowered, showed pink tinting over the front of Calderon's shirt, and jacket. Blood diluted by rainwater. It also showed a gash that started somewhere under Calderon's thick black hair and ended midway down his forehead. The body was limp and clammy.

Olmstead, bending far over to see better, uttered one word: 'Dead.'

Ralph took the lighter and moved it back and forth. He touched the purple wound on Calderon's forehead and bent lower to examine it. 'No,' he said softly. 'It's still bleeding. Dead people don't bleed.' He fished out the damp handkerchief and gently wiped dirt and blood from the ashen face. He twisted to look back towards the doorway. 'How did he get in here; that furnace-room door had to be locked from the *inside*.'

They looked at each other, an uneasy silence gripping them until Olmstead said, 'Well, if it *was* locked, then someone had to unlock it from down here, and if Calderon came through those storm-doors from outside, Ralph, he'd be the one who'd known the door wasn't locked . . . ' Olmstead didn't finish it; he didn't have to, for obviously the person who had previously unlocked the doors from *inside* the house would be the same person who'd entered the house that way.

'That doesn't make sense,' said McAuliffe. 'Look at his head. He'd have been unconscious when he came through the doors and into this room, wouldn't he?'

6

The Mystery Deepens

One thing was clear: Calderon wasn't dead. How he'd got inside — whether he'd staggered in after being savagely beaten over the head, or whether he'd been attacked *after* getting inside, was purest mystery, but the fact that he was alive made it probable that in good time he'd be able to explain everything.

The main issue at the moment, as McAuliffe said, was to get him upstairs where the fire was, and care for his wound.

It was while they were lifting him that Ralph discovered the automatic pistol was gone.

Getting the limp, soggy body up the stone stairs into that little butler's pantry took a bit of doing. Calderon kept slipping through their grip as though he were putty.

Ralph had his shoulders and Mackenzie McAuliffe had his legs. Frank Olmstead brought up the rear holding McAuliffe's cigarette lighter, which was actually no longer needed once they'd got back into the main cellar beneath the house.

It was almost as difficult getting their burden clear of the small pantry too, but after that had been accomplished it was a relatively simple matter getting back to the living-room, where a great, crackling fire was bringing warmth back to the room.

Betty and Mary-Katherine were stunned. In fact, Mary-Katherine recoiled from the gruesome sight Calderon presented and backed away while the grimly silent men struggled towards the hearth. Betty grabbed up several cushions and a neatly folded robe that had been lying upon a long love-seat. With these she made a pallet near the fireplace where Calderon was gently lowered.

Mackenzie stood up wiping his hands while the others hovered over the unconscious man. He turned, went to the bar and quarter-filled an amber glass with straight whisky which he took back and handed Ralph, who was kneeling beside the sodden figure. He then said, 'Betty, we'll need some towels and some kind of disinfectant. He got that dirt off the floor in the cellar.'

Betty straightened up nodding. She took Mary-Katherine with her and hastened towards the rear of the house.

The men made certain Calderon was comfortable and that the fire would warm him, then there was little else they could do for the moment, so Olmstead fished forth one of his cigars, bit it savagely and lighted up. Ralph got tiredly to his feet and examined the bloody water on his trousers and coat.

Mackenzie said, 'He couldn't have got into that room by himself if he was knocked over the head outside.'

Olmstead smoked and narrowly eyed McAuliffe. But he had nothing to say. Neither did Ralph, who stood above the unconscious man looking pensive and rumpled.

The sounds of the storm washed over the house in waves, sometimes striking from the north, sometimes from east or west, as though the wind were out of control. Rainwater made its endless cacophony too, but these sounds had been part of this long night since its beginning, and so were more or less accepted by the inmates of Masters Manor. Or possibly the other, infinitely more brutal things that were happening closed the minds of those people to the storm.

Betty returned. She and Mary-Katherine had gone upstairs to Calderon's room and had brought down fresh, dry clothing along with some bandaging material, some warm water in a bowl, and a bottle of household disinfectant. Betty had also slipped into a pair of loose-fitting dark slacks and a sweater, both of which made her look more gaunt than ever.

She was capable, though, and the others stood back to let her work over the injured man. Her husband helped remove his jacket and shirt, helped her get him dried off and dressed in the dry clothing, but otherwise Betty McAuliffe did all the work. Mary-Katherine seemed to want to help, but each time a towel or a soggy bandage glistened bloodily by firelight Mary-Katherine recoiled.

Mackenzie and Olmstead moved over to where Ralph was impassively standing, wet clothes to the blazing fire. The men were grim and glum. Olmstead said in a subdued voice that if, as McAuliffe had said, Calderon had been attacked *outside*, it had to also follow that McAuliffe's other theory was correct: The man couldn't, with his scalp split wide open, have lifted one of those heavy storm-doors and got inside, because he wouldn't have been conscious.

'So,' he concluded, 'that means someone *brought* him inside and dumped him in that dark room perhaps figuring no one would find him there.' Olmstead paused, looked at his small audience, then shrugged. '*Why* anyone would go to all that trouble I haven't the faintest idea — it seems to me that if someone had simply wanted Calderon knocked out, he'd have left him where he fell after attacking him . . . Unless of course he was afraid someone might see the body lying out there — improbable, at least tonight when it's so damned black out. But in any case, my point is — whoever carried Calderon inside and dumped him in that cellar-room, is now *inside* the house.'

Olmstead drew in a mouthful of smoke and let it trickle back out again. McAuliffe and Ralph kept looking at him. Finally, Ralph looked over where Betty was briskly at work, and said, 'Until he comes round we won't know.'

'His gun is gone,' McAuliffe muttered, then turned. 'Ralph, are there other guns in the house?'

'In the study,' said Ralph. 'Come along.'

The men went in where the cold corpse of Hugh Fielding lay. Someone had mercifully drawn a dark grey blanket over the body. Betty McAuliffe no doubt, since none of the men had been upstairs lately and since Mary-Katherine had demonstrated an obvious and marked aversion to going anywhere near the dead man.

The guns were revolvers, unlike the automatic Calderon'd had. There were four of them in a desk-drawer. Two were handsomely engraved. They'd been presented to his father, Hugh explained, by wealthy clients Hugh had brought to Masters Manor for target-shooting. Olmstead flipped out the cylinder of the engraved pistol Ralph handed him. It was empty. Ralph rummaged, came up with a carton of steel-jacketed bullets and put them on the desk.

McAuliffe's gun was also unloaded. It had evidently never been fired. The weapon Ralph took was a somewhat worn old revolver with a target-length barrel. He seemed familiar with this gun, so when Olmstead said a bit drily, he'd never before known anyone who kept a veritable arsenal in his desk, Ralph explained that there being no gun-closet in the entire house, his father had simply dumped the weapons in that unused desk drawer, and would allow his son to use only the long-barrelled pistol he now was loading, until Ralph had achieved maturity.

They had all seen the section of the main cellar where an indoor target-range had been set up, along the east wall, and Ralph told them that as a youth, on long, bitter winter days he, sometimes with his father, used to go down there and target-practise. Ralph held forth the old weapon in his hand. 'This was the only one I could even come close to equalling him with. He was a phenomenally good pistol-shot.'

Olmstead smoked and considered the gun he was holding, then said, 'I'm not. I've seen my share of what these things do to people. I've never had any desire to take them up as a hobby.'

McAuliffe reached and lifted the telephone. It gave back absolutely no sound at all, no dialing tone, no buzzing or clicking. The line was as dead as it had ever been.

They tucked the weapons out of sight and returned to the living-room where Calderon looked at least tolerably presentable. Mary-Katherine was alone by the fireplace, highball glass in hand, staring at the unconscious man. Mackenzie asked, with a quick harshness, where his wife was. Mrs. Olmstead smiled into his face. 'Went to wash up. She was a mess.'

Mackenzie at once started briskly across towards the stairway, but before he reached it Betty appeared at the upper landing on her way down. Mackenzie's shoulders loosened and slumped. He waited, then accompanied his wife back to the fireplace where Olmstead was speaking, his voice hard and droning, not at all pleasant nor reassuring.

'. . . Got to be some kind of maniac, and if he is *inside* this house we've either got to find him and do whatever is necessary, or we've got to take our chances out in the storm.'

Olmstead glanced swiftly towards the shadowy, dark stairway. He then glanced towards the doorway beyond the large dining-room where access gave way to the kitchen and the several porches, pantries and back-rooms. The eyes of the others followed Olmstead's lead and sought out those places. Mary-Katherine gulped the last of her drink and raised up to set the empty glass on top of the oaken mantle. She looked flushed and moderately drunk.

Ralph said, 'I'm not saying he didn't come inside, but I'm suggesting that if murder were still his motive, he could have caught the three of us down in the cellar, or he could have caught the women when they were alone up here at the bar.

Olmstead gazed steadily at Ralph. 'Okay. I'll buy that. Now perhaps you can tell us just what in the hell he *does* want here; what his motive is. I swear to God, Ralph, this is the craziest house I've ever been in, in my life.'

Ralph's gaze darkened towards the older man, but Mackenzie McAuliffe broke in saying. 'What's the house got to do with it? If there's a madman out in the night trying to murder people — or if he's inside the house — then the thing we've got to do is find him and finish him off.'

Calderon groaned loudly enough to be heard over in front of the fireplace. They all turned abruptly but only Betty moved. She went over and sank down beside the injured man, lay a cool hand upon his temple, then said, 'Ken, help me get a little of the whisky down him.'

They all moved up. Mackenzie gently raised the wounded man's head. His wife got a swallow down, then another swallow. Emilio's eyes flickered, opened wide and closed from lamp-glare. Ralph moved quickly and switched off an end-table lamp that had shone directly into the wounded man's face.

Calderon swallowed another sip of the fiery whisky. He looked up, eyes rolling aimlessly, then he sank back against Mackenzie's arms and sighed, going all limp again.

Mary-Katherine said, 'Say, how do you know he doesn't have a brain-concussion? He might even be haemorrhaging inside his head. What he needs is a damned good doctor.'

Her husband turned a sardonic smile upon her, but said nothing.

Betty looked at her husband and gently smiled. It was a special little private interlude for them. He smiled back. They were together and *that* mattered, evidently.

Calderon moaned again and this time when his heavy lids raised, he looked directly up at Ralph with recognition. His lips moved. Betty dropped down. The others crowded up close. Frank Olmstead, dead cigar clamped in his mouth, stood back staring, expressionless and blank-eyed.

Ralph knelt to hear. Calderon said, 'Two of them . . . I saw them at the cars . . . I drew the gun . . . They disappeared in the darkness . . . I went forward. One came from behind. I didn't see him — I heard him . . . ' Calderon tried feebly to raise a hand to his head. 'Headache . . . ' The hand fell back and he let weighted lids drop. He stirred weakly as though to change position on the pallet and Betty helped until he was comfortable, then she drew back and looked upwards at Ralph.

Olmstead said softly, bleakly, 'Okay, there are two maniacs out there. Or there are two *inside this damned house*. That makes all the difference in the world. Someone's got to go for the police.'

Mackenzie said, 'Any suggestions about

just how we do that? You heard what he said. They were doing something with our cars. Putting them out of commission, obviously, so what is your suggestion as to how we get away from here?'

The antagonism in McAuliffe's voice was so noticeable Betty looked at him and said, 'Ken, can't we just get along a while longer?' It was the way she said it, her musical, velvety voice making the words seem warmly entreating, that made McAuliffe look a moment, then smile at her. He said no more.

Ralph sounded baffled. 'But why? Who are they; what do they want? Why did they shoot my father and what is their purpose in marooning us here by putting the cars out of order?'

Mary-Katherine didn't answer any of the questions but she said something that made them all look intently at her.

'Hey, I'll make a wager no tree fell across that telephone line, folks. I'll bet our bloody-minded friends out there deliberately broke the line.'

Mary-Katherine gave them all a big, vacuous smile.

7

After the Last Raindrop

Emilio began to perspire and shake so they made a bed for him on one of the sofas of the living-room, pushed it up so that the back was close to the fireplace, covered him with blankets and stood helplessly by as his tremors seemed to get worse. The heat passing into and through the back of the sofa would help if anything at all could help. Olmstead said it looked to him as though poor Calderon had caught a bad chill out there; that with his loss of blood and lowered resistance it'd be a cussed wonder if Calderon didn't go into pneumonia. Olmstead also said, 'We can't just leave the man here to die, can we?'

Ralph said Emilio seemed to be getting better, not worse, and Olmstead snorted derisively. 'Look at him shake; you call that getting better, damn it all?'

Mackenzie, only half heeding this little exchange, mentioned something else. 'I don't like the idea of those men being in the house, perhaps waiting to get a good shot at one of us. Olmstead, Ralph, we're armed. I think we'd better force the issue before they pick us off one at a time like rats in a rainbarrel.'

Olmstead seemed to hang back, but when Ralph nodded and turned as though to lead their little expedition, Olmstead went along. Then, at the doorway leading into the kitchen he said, 'Wait a minute; what assurance do we have these madmen won't shoot the women?'

If there was an answer no one gave it. Betty looked at her husband without comment and Mary-Katherine, sitting relaxed in a large maroon leather chair, waved an arm. 'Hell; might as well be all-shot as half-shot. Don't worry about us anyway. You just *think* the day of chivalry is dead.'

Olmstead gazed at his wife, then turned and jerked his head. 'Let's go, Ralph.' He was red in the face.

It was Mackenzie who broke up their trio by announcing that he would stay with the women. Ralph and Olmstead turned and went on through into the back of the house.

The possibilities for concealment in Masters Manor were almost limitless and Ralph frankly admitted this when he and Olmstead were in the large kitchen again. Olmstead was curious about secret panels and closets, but Ralph disillusioned him on that score. As far as he'd ever heard there'd never been any such things built into the old stone mansion, and if *he* didn't know of them then it was very unlikely that anyone else would know of them, particularly strangers, as he assumed those men were who had killed his father and who had come within inches of also killing Emilio Calderon.

They made a closet-by-closet search, one standing pistol in hand, while the other one searched, then trading off. It took time; the house was large and roomy. When they'd finished downstairs and were upstairs, Ralph said, 'It doesn't make much sense, but perhaps they carried Calderon inside, left him, then went back outside again.'

Olmstead, quiet now for some time, made a grunt. 'And suppose Calderon unlocked that damned set of storm-doors himself; how would that work out?'

'Fine,' assented Ralph drily, 'except for one thing: Did he hit himself over the head?'

They finished upstairs and started down again. Now it seemed that the rain had stopped altogether, but until they'd passed through the living-room again, bound for that narrow pantry where the cellar door was, they had no occasion to know this. Then, in the pantry, they saw that the window was dry.

The wind increased though; it tore at the house with destructive force making Olmstead remark that he preferred rain any day of the year to wind.

In the cellar they found everything as it had been when they'd passed through the rooms down there. The storm-doors in the furnace-room were still locked, the puddles made by someone crossing through to where Calderon had been found, were still dark and slippery.

'Nothing,' said Ralph, coming out of the lightless store-room with its faintly aromatic fragrance of malt and mash. 'They aren't in the house.'

Olmstead appeared puzzled by that. 'Would they have shoved Calderon in here because they figured we might go out there to investigate, and find him?'

Ralph said, 'Maybe.'

Olmstead's eyes gleamed. 'Okay, then who unlocked those doors for them?'

Ralph gave his head a weary shake. 'I don't know. *I* didn't, but that's all I'm sure of. Perhaps Dubois didn't check them last night — or tonight — whichever it is. Let's go back upstairs.'

Olmstead caught Ralph's arm, detaining him. 'Where is your nearest neighbour?'

'One mile away, through the woods that border us to the north.' Ralph shook the detaining hand off. 'Forget it, Olmstead. It wouldn't be safe if there were only *one* killer out there, but with two of them, and watching the house, you wouldn't get a hundred yards. They'd team-up on you like they did Emilio.'

'Damnation, Ralph, sitting like this is worse than running a risk.'

'Not if you get killed running it, it isn't. Let's go back upstairs.' Ralph looked at his wrist and said, sounding amazed, 'It's only two o'clock. I'd have sworn it had to be closer to five.'

They rejoined the others by the fireplace, reported that they'd found nothing at all, and Betty told them Emilio had stopped shaking and appeared now to be in a deep sleep.

Mary-Katherine got out of her chair heading for the bar. Her husband headed her off, herded her back to the same chair and gave her a gentle push. She dropped down looking sulphurously at Olmstead.

The telephone rang.

It was such an unexpected sound everyone except Mary-Katherine jumped. Ralph whirled towards the study with the others following after — except Mary-Katherine who sat where she was facing the roaring fire, her back to the couch where Emilio Calderon lay, dry now, relaxed, bandaged and motionless.

The voice that came down the line to Ralph was masculine and agitated. 'Mister Fielding? We've been a couple of hours tracing the break in your line. It was in the woods north of the road about three-quarters of a mile from Manor House. Mister Fielding; someone cut it. Are you all right up there?'

'No,' said Ralph. 'Can you switch me over to the office of the State Police in the village?'

The agitated voice answered promptly. 'You'll have to dial it, Mister Fielding.' The man gave Ralph a telephone number then he said, 'Is there anything we can do, from down here?'

Ralph started to reply and the line went dead in his hand. He clicked the instrument and got no sound at all. He called into the mouthpiece several times more, then held the telephone away from his face. Frank Olmstead was staring at him. So were the others. Olmstead said, 'Who was it; what did he say, Ralph?'

'They found a break in the line over in

the forest. It had been cut. Deliberately cut. Then the telephone went dead again.'

'Yes, but what was that about the State Police?'

'He gave me their number.'

Olmstead looked at the McAuliffes and made a futile gesture with his hands. 'No better off than we were.' He turned and wandered back where his wife was still sitting, drowsily gazing into the fire. He watched her a moment then went on past towards the bar. She started to arise. Olmstead turned. 'Not you, lover; you're already half-loaded.'

The McAuliffes joined Olmstead at the bar. Ralph didn't, not at first. He went round the couch to bend over Calderon and feel the man's flushed face. It was hot to the touch. Calderon's eyes flickered open. He had a strange lustre to his black gaze. He tried to smile. 'Water,' he said, 'please.'

It had been lucidly said and perfectly pronounced, there was little trace of that earlier slur. Ralph patted Calderon's shoulder and headed for the kitchen.

When he returned the others were still hunched over bar-stools at the other end of the room. They paid little attention to Ralph.

Calderon drank greedily, then lay back breathing hard from the exertion. He waited a moment then raised a hand to his head. 'Bad?' he asked.

Ralph nodded. 'Bad enough. He must have hit you with a gun-barrel to make that kind of a split in your scalp. How's the headache?'

'Well, not really very bad now. But I'm drowsy. Weak in the joints . . . drowsy. Ralph . . . ?'

'Yes, Emilio?'

'Have you found them?'

Assuming Calderon meant the men who had struck him down Ralph shook his head. 'We think they are still outside. I think the safest thing is for us to stay inside with the doors locked, until daylight.'

Calderon's bright eyes turned feverishly baffled. 'You went outside and found me . . . ?'

Ralph explained: 'Someone brought

you inside through the cellar storm-doors, Emilio; we found you unconscious down there.'

'They — brought me inside?'

'Yes, Don't ask, Emilio, because I haven't the faintest idea why they did that. Tell me; did you get a look at them?'

'No. Not up close. They wore black rain suits, coats, trousers, hats. I ran ahead and they ran away. Ralph; what do they want here? If it was to kill your father, why are they still here — or are they — perhaps, after crippling the cars they have gone.'

Ralph said, 'And after crippling the telephone.'

'We should find out,' said Calderon, and raised a hand to his bandaged head again. 'Could I possibly have more water?'

Ralph went to fetch it. When he returned this time the Olmsteads and McAuliffes were gathered round Calderon's sofa. Mackenzie was speaking softly to the injured man, and obviously Calderon was listening only with a great effort.

Ralph helped him get the second glass of water down. Calderon then lay back, breathing hard again, gave them a little wan smile and closed his eyes. He seemed to drift away into slumber again as they watched; his entire body loosened and his features lost their expression of concerted physical effort.

Now, when the others returned to the bar, Ralph went with them. He explained something he hadn't mentioned before. 'That man from the telephone company — when he told me the telephone wire had been deliberately cut, he also asked if we were all right up here. I told him no, that we were not, and that I wanted to be connected with the State Police. That was when the line went dead again.'

'So,' said Mackenzie, 'the telephone-man knows there is trouble here.'

Olmstead, sipping a tall chilled drink, was listening, but he was also watching his wife who had, despite his earlier admonition, got herself another highball. But it was Olmstead who spoke next, saying that if the telephone-man were alerted, it would perhaps be only a matter of an hour or so before the police arrived — providing of course the storm hadn't washed out a bridge or a length of the roadway.

This all tended to lift their spirits a little. Betty slid off her stool to go look at her patient. Her husband, fondly watching her cross the room, said, 'We've had all we need for one night of horror anyway,' and turned to lean upon the bar regarding Ralph. 'None of it makes any sense, though.'

If Ralph was supposed to make an enlightening comment, he must have disappointed Mackenzie McAuliffe by remaining thoughtfully silent. Frank Olmstead excused himself to go upstairs and shave. Evidently things seemed that safe and normal to him again.

Mary-Katherine, watching her husband's thick body go up towards the second-floor landing, smirked. 'He never gets drunk. Isn't that the most disgusting gawddamned thing you ever heard of? Tycoon Frank Olmstead always keeps his cool head. You know, I think if my aged and loving husband were to cut himself up there shaving, he'd damned well bleed icewater,' Mary-Katherine shoved her emptied glass at Ralph and raised those beautiful large eyes half in challenge. Ralph took the glass without any hesitation, put it on the shelf below the bartop, filled it with harmless, non-intoxicating quinine-water and smilingly handed it back.

Mary-Katherine knocked back a big swallow and said, 'You're sweet, Ralph. 'You know how many really sweet men there are in this stinking, lousy damned world? I'll tell you: Just one. You, love. Come round here and sit beside me. Old icewater won't be back for a minute; I need some comforting.'

Betty looked at Ralph with wry amusement from over beside Calderon's couch where the younger woman's voice had carried easily. She gently lifted and dropped her shoulders. It took all kinds to make up a world, that gesture seemed to say, and who would have it otherwise — even though at times such a situation could cause irritation.

8

A Lie!

When Mary-Katherine's husband returned from upstairs he looked quite respectable, not like someone routed out of bed by a murder and kept on his feet afterwards out of fear of another murder.

He took his wife away from the bar and into the kitchen where he said they would make a pot of coffee. Everyone, he said, needed a big cup of black coffee.

It was difficult to imagine the variety of logic behind that statement. They'd all been drinking so they needed no pick-me-up, none were likely to fall asleep — not many people did that with murder hanging over their heads — and otherwise coffee didn't serve much purpose.

Still, no one protested when Olmstead took his wife away, and at least one of them, Betty McAuliffe made an observation that may have been pertinent.

She said, 'Well; if I have to drink a cup of coffee to sober *her* up, I'll make the sacrifice.'

The McAuliffes and Ralph Fielding went over to Emilio's sofa and looked. Calderon was sleeping like a baby. Betty lay a gentle hand upon his neck, upon his cheek. 'I do believe he's improving. Maybe that shaking, that feverish look, wasn't really a prelude to something.'

Ralph had a confession to make. 'I put a couple of aspirin in his water. It's about all I knew of that would help.'

Mackenzie went to a front window and looked out. The rain had definitely stopped although stygian clouds hung overhead so low one could see their constant black writhing.

The wind seemed to possess a life-force and a direction of its own, suspended somewhere between rooftop and sky. Within that area it ran and turned, swooped and hurled upwards, fell like invisible lead to push upon the house making it groan, and it whipped round the corner into that recessed place where the front door stood, making a sobbing sound, an undulating whimper.

Mackenzie turned back towards the fireplace where the others mutely stood. 'What an incredible night this has been,' he said. 'Listen to that wind.'

He lit a cigarette and smiled at both his wife and Ralph. The wood in the fireplace had burned down somewhat. It wasn't actually chilly in the huge room but those sounds Mackenzie had mentioned made it seem cold. Wind had the ability to do that.

The house, with its huge forced-air furnace, was never allowed to get cold; the heat throughout was thermostatically controlled day and night. Still, as the firelight had diminished considerably, Ralph went to the woodbox. There was little in there but kindling. He headed for the kitchen saying there were logs stacked along the rear wall outside the door, that he'd fetch a couple back.

The coffee pot was merrily perking on the electric range, the kitchen lights were on, there was the strong scent of tobacco-smoke in the kitchen but neither of the Olmsteads were there.

Ralph looked round, thought they might be in the adjoining sunroom and went through to the back door, unlocked it, opened it and reached for the logs piled neatly and conveniently out there. They were slippery so he had to step across the cement approach to use both hands. Something caught his attention. He turned quickly, feeling hair along the nape of his neck rising.

But it wasn't some evil shape looming threateningly, it was a light, yellow and none too strong, winking off and on from an upstairs window. He stepped forth and leaned for a better look. The light went out and did not reappear. He waited, the wind ruffled his hair, pushed cold fingers down his neck, tore at him from two directions at the same time but the light did not show again.

He took two logs and went back inside, kicked the door closed, balanced both logs precariously on one arm while he turned the lock, then he returned to the living-room where Betty said the wind must be strong, out there to muss his hair that way.

He nodded mechanically, fed the fire, made certain the logs were properly behind the andirons, then fished forth a comb and put his hair back in shape, all without saying anything.

Calderon called softly. Betty at once went round his sofa and bent down. Ralph said, 'Mackenzie, would you say it could be possible that someone here in the house could be working with those murderers out there?'

McAuliffe, smoking a small cigarette, flipped the thing into the fireplace and raised thoughtful eyes. 'What did you see out there?' When Ralph didn't answer right away McAuliffe leaned a little. 'Where are the Olmsteads?'

'They weren't in the kitchen.'

'Was the back-door locked?'

'Yes. But when I went out for the logs there was someone upstairs making what looked like blinker signals with a flashlight from one of the windows.'

McAuliffe kept leaning and looking intently at Ralph. He said, 'From the Olmsteads' room?'

'No. From *your* room.'

McAuliffe slowly straightened up. 'Ralph, neither Betty nor I went five feet from this fireplace while you were gone.'

Ralph hadn't thought they had; no one could have run upstairs, made those signals, run back down again during the short moments it had taken Ralph to re-lock the back-door and step through into the living-room.

McAuliffe glanced towards the kitchen door, visible beyond the dining-room's arched passageway. 'Did you look around; I thought they'd be in there, Olmstead trying to get black coffee down his wife.'

Ralph didn't answer right away, and a moment later the kitchen door swung open and Mary-Katherine appeared bearing a tray with cups, saucers, spoons, with cream and sugar. Behind her, holding the hot pot with a wadded-up dish-towel, came her husband. Mary-Katherine was smiling; apparently, if Frank had got any black coffee down her, it either hadn't been enough or else it hadn't had time to work. She went to a table near the fireplace, set the tray there and said, 'Come share the bounty of Masters Manor, friends — or enemies, whichever we all are.'

Frank unsmilingly and methodically placed cups on saucers and poured. Betty, who got the first cup, tamed it with cream, which also cooled it, and took the cup over to Calderon's sofa. The others accepted cups from Mary-Katherine and no one had much to say.

Olmstead, watching Ralph, seemed suddenly very interested. He strolled over to take a position between Fielding and McAuliffe, backsides to the roaring fire. 'You've thought of something,' he said, making a statement of it. 'You've figured some way out of this maze.'

It was about as far from what Ralph actually was thinking as Olmstead could have got, but he didn't know that. Betty's low, gentle laugh came from over in front of the sofa where she was helping Emilio sip the coffee. The sound attracted Mary-Katherine, who took her own cup and walked over there.

Ralph watched the women from sombre eyes. Olmstead persisted. 'Well, what is it, Ralph? If it's a means for getting out of this crazy place, let's hear it.'

Ralph turned slightly. He and Frank Olmstead were the same size, both were big-boned men, but Olmstead carried considerably more weight than Ralph, and of course he was older. Right now, that patina of confident self-sufficiency held his faintly coarse, shrewd features in a mould of quiet dominance while he waited for the younger man to obey his invocation.

Ralph said, 'What do you suppose the chances are that one or both of those murderers are in the house?'

McAuliffe, understanding, shot Ralph a look, then let his gaze drift past to the dark stairway. Ralph was trying to settle in his own mind whether Olmstead had made those signals upstairs, or whether one of the unknown killers had. It was a gallant thing to do, give Olmstead the benefit of the doubt, but it wasn't very practical since he knew perfectly well the Olmsteads hadn't been in the kitchen when those signals were given. McAuliffe's expression, when it dropped back to Ralph's face, seemed to imply that gallantry was admirable, but not now, not with lives at stake.

Olmstead's reply to Ralph's question was a hard and emphatic wag of the head. 'Not a chance, Ralph. If they were in here we'd have known it by now.'

'How?' demanded Ralph.

'Well, they'd probably have shot another of us. Or cracked someone's skull like they did for Calderon . . . No; I'd say they wouldn't be in here.'

McAuliffe, watching Ralph, saw the slight narrowing of the younger man's gaze. 'They might have slipped in through the kitchen windows; they're not too new and the latches aren't tamper-proof.'

Olmstead gave his head another of those emphatic, negative shakes. 'Not while Mary-Katherine and I were in there, just now, and not before we went out there either.'

'How could you be sure?' Ralph persisted.

'How?' exclaimed Olmstead, showing

exasperation. 'Because I checked the latches when we went out there, and because we were in the room all the while afterwards. That's how. Ralph; it's getting to you. Get hold of yourself, boy.'

McAuliffe turned gently and sought out his wife over by Calderon's sofa. He didn't say anything. Neither did Ralph for a moment. Then he finished his coffee and went to the tray for a refill.

Frank Olmstead had lied!

Afterwards Ralph returned to the fireplace, put his back to the heat and said, 'What I simply can't comprehend is the *reason* . . . .' He said that so softly only the two men heard, and there was genuine amazement in his voice, in his eyes.

Olmstead rocked back and forth on his toes and heels. He finished his coffee and turned to set the cup on the high oaken mantle. Then he fished around inside a coat pocket for one of his cigars, lit it and stood with his companions, watching the two women.

Calderon seemed much better; it was actually a somewhat miraculous recovery. The man had to possess enormous reserves of stamina and energy to come along so well and so fast. His experience had been traumatic to say the least. Very probably there wasn't another person among his companions who would have been able to sit up so soon after being so savagely beaten and wounded, but sit up he did, with Betty McAuliffe's help. He even smiled at Mary-Katherine, who smiled back, and whose husband saw her smile back. She went after some whisky to mix into Calderon's coffee. While she was at the bar she also managed to hoist a quick, straight one, for herself. Her husband also saw that, no doubt.

McAuliffe suddenly said, 'Not again,' and pointed. Across the room the front windows were streaked with water, it was raining. He also said a quiet, mild curse.

But the rain didn't last. It came and went, more in the manner of a squall than of a rainstorm. The wind didn't stop; it didn't even diminish. It still seemed to break out of all directions simultaneously and hurl itself upon the house making eerie sounds.

Ralph excused himself to go wash and shave. It was, he reminded the others, almost four in the morning. He also said, looking past Olmstead at Mackenzie McAuliffe, that the police would surely be arriving soon. If that announcement had been made so that Ralph might catch some flicker of trepidation from Olmstead from the corner of Ralph's eye, it was a complete failure. Olmstead was watching his wife, didn't seem to even hear what had been said, and had his teeth clamped down upon his cigar.

McAuliffe suddenly stepped past to put his coffee cup on the tray and announce that he too ought to go up and make himself presentable. As though to emphasise his point McAuliffe rubbed a hand over his whiskery jaw. The two of them walked away towards the stairs. Olmstead said something in a dry voice to his wife, who was pouring whisky into Calderon's upheld cup. She ignored him completely.

The lights flickered and for five seconds everyone singled out one lamp to watch. No one moved. Even the two men halfway up the stairs stopped to turn and wait.

But evidently whatever interruption had caused that momentary flicker was insufficient to break the circuit because the lights regained their steady brightness and did not flicker again.

'That damned lousy wind,' muttered McAuliffe. 'I'd rather have rain.'

He and Ralph resumed their way upstairs where hall lights, and even several bedroom lights, visible through ajar doors, dispelled the gloom except in corners, and also except in that short, gloomy little passageway that led to the rusty old fire-escape.

McAuliffe showed no surprise when Ralph, instead of continuing along to his own quarters, stopped at the door of the room the McAuliffes had shared, and went on in.

Across the room, almost directly opposite the door, were two large windows, marred now with beads of water that exploded against the glass when gusts of wind broke and scattered them.

'Are you sure?' McAuliffe asked.

Ralph nodded. He was sure those blinking lights had come from those windows; after all, he'd grown up in this house. Even on a dismal, dark and stormy night he wasn't likely to make that kind of mistake.

9

The Shank of the Night

All that was discernible from the McAuliffes' window was wet and endless blackness. That writhing sooty sky had no pale streaks anywhere even though dawn couldn't be far off.

But Ralph, who was familiar with everything hereabouts, said, 'A light from up here, if someone was watching, would be visible quite a distance. Beyond the garden are some meadows, and beyond them are the trees, the patch of old forest we and our neighbour to the north and west have always preserved as a means for ensuring privacy and also as a game preserve. I doubt that anyone as far as the forest would be able to see a light on a night like this. At least not without binoculars. But anyone closer, say a quarter mile off, would be able to see, even though the light I saw wasn't very strong. The trick would be to know when to watch this window.'

Mackenzie made a correction. 'The trick would be to know what the signal meant.' He looked at the carpet, at the sill, then around the room at his, and his wife's, effects. Nothing seemed disturbed. 'He was taking a chance, using this room.'

Ralph turned. 'I think not. *You* or your wife were the ones in danger. Suppose either of you had walked in here and caught him signalling.'

'I see your point,' murmured McAuliffe, and went to get a razor off a small table. 'If we waste much more time up here they'll all start wondering.'

Ralph left the room, went along to his own quarters and prepared to shower, to shave and eventually to redress. While he was at it the lights flickered again but recovered as they'd done before. It was one of those little interludes that shakes one's confidence in the huge and enormously efficient man-made and man-operated public utility facilities.

Ralph had a cigarette while he was

dressing and from time to time eyed the lamp. Finally, philosophical about the matter, he slipped into a casual coat, killed his smoke in an ashtray and returned to the hallway.

Mackenzie was already waiting, his bedroom door open, standing pensively by that enigmatic window. He turned at the sound of Ralph's entrance and said, 'What, exactly, was Olmstead's connection with your father — if you don't mind my asking.'

Ralph didn't quite know. 'The last words my father and I had touched upon that, but all he said was that Olmstead was some sort of associate. That could mean anything; that my father was representing Olmstead through his ad agency, or that Olmstead and my father were involved in some business deal apart from the agency.'

Mackenzie moved slowly from the window towards the door. 'Olmstead isn't your father's type. That's what I've been wondering about. Where was the common ground; what was the basis for their friendship — if it *was* friendship, and

I can't imagine Hugh inviting someone to his home if he didn't like them.'

Ralph said, 'I wondered about those things earlier, and I thought I had a good way of getting all the answers. Then that damned telephone went out.'

'Olmstead again?' asked Mackenzie. 'Part of whatever made him signal someone? Why did he signal?'

Ralph shoved fisted hands deep into trouser pockets as he answered. 'If you recall, Mackenzie, it was very shortly after I spilled the beans about that telephone-man getting the police started up here, that Olmstead decided he had to come upstairs to shave.'

'And he shaved.'

'All right. What else did he do? And as soon as he came back down, he took his wife out into the kitchen. Then they both disappeared. Up here, of course, because I saw the light-signals. Later, he told a deliberate lie.'

McAuliffe stepped out into the lighted hall and looked both ways, then twisted to face Ralph. 'What was this way of getting the answers you mentioned?'

'Telephoning down to New York to my father's secretary, or his chief administrative assistant. Either one of them would know if Olmstead and my father were involved in anything together.'

Mackenzie said, 'Well, that's out, isn't it? We'd better get back down there. As for the other thing — you think he signalled for someone to pull out, because the police are on their way?' Mackenzie didn't await an answer. 'It is likely at that,' he said.

They descended the stairs together. The others were sitting somewhat awkwardly, stiffly, around the fireplace. The mood seemed slightly ugly. It wasn't anything Ralph or Mackenzie could put a finger on, but there was a feeling of leashed violence in the atmosphere.

Emilio was back asleep again. Ralph went to look at him. Calderon's skin was quite pale but his beard was very black. He was one of those Nixon-type individuals who, if they didn't shave at least twice daily, resembled a full-blown private.

Betty said in her soothing voice, 'He's doing amazingly well. I got him some aspirin from the kitchen.'

Mary-Katherine spoke, and at once Mackenzie and Ralph understood why her husband was sitting like a dangerous Buddha, silent and malevolent, gazing straight at her. Mary-Katherine had been at the bar again. She was much farther along the route to drunkeness now than she'd been before Ralph and Mackenzie had gone upstairs.

She said, 'Krysake, he got hit over the head. You people want to give him a medal? I bet if I could have him alone for an hour I could fling him back to you a damned sight weaker'n he is from that gun-barrel over the head. Hey, Ralphie-boy, what this stinkin' party needs is a little more life — a good kick in the seat of the pants, Ralphie-boy. How about drinks all round, Ralphie-boy?'

No one answered and Frank Olmstead very slowly got up out of his chair. The others waited, expecting the large man to explode. But he didn't, he simply went over and pulled his wife to her feet, and steered her, unresisting, towards the kitchen. Over his shoulder he said, 'Coffee'll do it.'

When the Olmsteads were gone Betty said, 'They went at one another like tigers while you were gone, Ken. It was embarrassing.' She thought a moment then said, 'It was also very enlightening. I've never before heard a woman swear like a man.'

Ralph asked if Olmstead had left the room while he and Mackenzie had been upstairs. Betty said that he had not left the room. Then she said, looking from one of them to the other, 'Why? What is it? Have you discovered something?'

The lights went out.

There was no warning, no flicker, no wavering or diminishing brightness. One minute there was light. The next minute there was darkness again, and it was much worse than it had been earlier because none of them were in the least prepared. They'd put aside their candles in careless confidence.

And Mackenzie didn't answer his wife, he went groping by firelight for a candle.

He'd put two aside in the study and went in there after them. When he returned, lighted the candles and found places to put them, he looked around then said, 'Where is Ralph?'

His wife had no answer but she left her chair in a rush and ran over to be close to McAuliffe.

It wasn't really very dark in the living-room even without the candles. The fireplace was popping merrily. But after the brilliance of at least a dozen lamps scattered around the huge living-room, firelight abetted by two demure candles made it seem quite dark and quite gloomy.

Ralph was nowhere in sight for the best of all reasons. It had struck him forcibly that again, when the Olmsteads were out of view, something happened. He had rushed to the kitchen.

But the scene out there was unmistakably authentic — shocking, but authentic. Evidently Mary-Katherine had been in the act of drinking hot black coffee at the insistence of her husband, at the precise moment when the lights failed.

Startled and none too steady anyway, she had upset the contents of the cup down the front of her dress. When Ralph burst into the room Frank was lighting a candle, possibly from a shelf or just as possibly from a pocket, and Mary-Katherine was giving a most electrifying demonstration of that ability she had for swearing. She was standing there, doused with hot coffee, swearing at the top of her voice.

At the sight of Ralph she whirled. 'Well what in the hell are you doing, hurtling through doors like that? I'll tell you what I wish, Ralph Fielding. I wish you and this gawddamned horror-chamber of a rockpile you got the nerve to call a house was shoved right up . . . '

'Mary-Katherine!' Olmstead stepped up with a large hand ominously raised to strike. 'Close your mouth! What's a little spilt coffee? Anyway, it was your own damned clumsiness. Go upstairs and change.'

'I won't!' She spat at her husband, placed both hands upon her hips and took a wide stance. 'Try an' make me!'

The hand moved with the speed of a striking snake. The blow popped, making a high, explosive sound, like a fire-cracker, but Mary-Katherine's head hardly rocked, her great mane of coppery hair scarcely vibrated. Obviously, Frank Olmstead had a perfected technique for slapping. Ralph, standing as though he'd taken root, watched Mary-Katherine. Tears welled into her eyes, her heavy mouth drooped, she slid both hands off her hips. Ralph thought she was going to collapse with hysterical sobs. Instead she turned and dutifully headed for the back stairway leading to the second floor.

Olmstead, motionless and looking slightly ridiculous with a candle in one hand, said, 'I'm sorry you had to see that. She's one of those people who either won't stop or can't stop after the first one.' He poured wax upon a saucer and set the candle there with great care, as though that were the most important thing in life to him. He turned back. 'Well, everybody's got some kind of cross to bear — you've just seen mine.' He made a poor smile.

'She'll be down in a little bit, and it'll all be forgotten. She'll be all right.'

Ralph, with nothing to say, nodded and turned to leave the room. It seemed preposterous now, in the face of that private crisis he'd vividly witnessed, to think Olmstead had somehow found the back-porch fuse box and caused the black-out. He wouldn't have had the time.

Which probably meant that the theory he and Mackenzie McAuliffe had worked out, about Olmstead signalling his friends the murderers to clear out, either was wrong, or the murderers hadn't got the signal and were still out there, capable of cutting the power-lines.

Or — there had been no signal; Olmstead had been searching McAuliffe's room for something. That was a fresh and intriguing thought. Ralph kept it and turned it over and over as he returned to the living-room to find Emilio sitting up smoking a cigarette, with Betty beside him holding a tinkling glass, evidently for Calderon since Ralph had noticed that Betty McAuliffe was a very sparing drinker.

Her husband was not in the living-room.

Ralph went around to smile at Calderon, but when he spoke he looked at Betty. He asked where Mackenzie was. She jerked her head in the direction of the study. 'In there trying to coax life out of the telephone.'

Emilio said, 'Ralph, what is it all about; who are those men out in the night? What do they want, and why don't they want any of us to leave your house?'

There were no answers, which Calderon evidently already knew, because instead of awaiting an answer he took the highball glass from Betty's hand, tipped up his bandaged head and let the cold, biting liquid run straight down. Then he said, 'I don't understand why, whoever they are, they returned me to the house. And if as Betty has been saying, somone unlocked the doors in the cellar from the inside — who was it?' Calderon's black eyes studied Ralph a moment then he said,

'I? You think it was I down there who opened the doors? But what for?'

Ralph had to softly smile at Calderon's vehemence, at his quick-splashing words that permitted no interruption. From across the room Mackenzie appeared in the gloomy study doorway beckoning. Ralph spun away without giving Calderon a second glance. If the telephone were functioning again he meant, this time, to make every second count before the service could be interrupted.

But it wasn't the telephone at all. Mackenzie took Ralph across the dark and brooding study to a leaded front window and said, 'Look down there to the left. Aren't those car lights?'

It seemed he was correct, but the distance, the whipping intervening tree-limbs, the utter blackness all round, made it impossible to be certain.

A voice from the doorway said, 'What do you see?' Olmstead strode across to join the other two and push his face close to the cold, streaked window panes. 'I don't see anything out there.'

Ralph and Mackenzie peered again and

were rewarded only by that deadly-same utter darkness. If it had been a car it had doused its lamps, or perhaps it had only been an illusion from the start.

Olmstead went to the telephone, hoisted it, listened a moment then put it down. 'Dead,' he muttered. 'Sometimes I get the feeling everything in this house is dead, or soon will be.'

He walked back into the living-room without a glance back at Mackenzie and Ralph.

10

Into the Storm

Something struck the north end of the house with great force, frightening the occupants enough to bring Olmstead from the kitchen and, moments later, to also bring his wife hastily down the stairway. She was freshly made-up and dressed in a strikingly handsome knitted suit that flattered her figure, although it neither needed flattering nor for the time being did any of the men notice.

Ralph ran into the study with Mackenzie behind him. Frank Olmstead made one of those slow starts of his, then turned back as though he thought someone should stay with the women.

Beyond the study with its grisly blanket-shrouded corpse of the late Hugh Fielding, there was a large closet, book-filled and smelling of ancient dust. Beyond that, but accessible only through the sunroom, which had an intervening doorway from the study, was an unused small room Ralph told Mackenzie had once been servant's quarters. This northern wall was also the limit of the house. In the darkness it was difficult to see anything in here so they returned to the sunroom and Mackenzie, standing by a floor-to-ceiling thick panel of glass, pointed out into the yard. The top of a tree was visible out there, but instead of standing erect, it was lying full length across the garden.

'Rain weakened the ground and the wind toppled it over,' suggested Mackenzie. 'It sounded like a — I don't know what.'

'Crashing aeroplane,' murmered Ralph, straining to see into the night. As he pulled back a flicker of gusty light appeared behind them. Betty's face, above her candle, looked deathly and cadaverous, her natural thinness was accentuated. She asked in a husky tone of voice what had happened outside. They told her a tree had been uprooted, had evidently struck the house and had bounced off.

She nodded, accepting this. 'Thank

God the house is stone,' she said, and waited for them to cross the room to her side. Her hand sought her husband's fingers below the flickering light. 'How much longer do we have to hang on?' she whispered, and Mackenzie reached up to place an arm around her shoulders.

'Not much longer. I think we've weathered the worst of it.'

She was looking over their shoulders back towards that plate window. She stiffened. 'A light. A light out there.' The men whirled. This time it definitely *was* a light, but Ralph had an explanation.

'That's from the staff quarters. Dubois will be getting up.' He glanced at his watch as though to confirm this when Mackenzie spoke.

'They'll shoot him, Ralph. The minute he steps out, over there and starts towards the manor house, they'll think he's one of us and shoot him.'

It seemed plausible if for no other reason than because they did not know how those men out there operated, what motivated them or what their purpose was. Ralph's eyes flickered for a second, then turned quiet again. 'Can't even 'phone him,' he muttered.

Mackenzie looked away from his wife. 'It's not very far,' he said, and Betty at once interjected a protest.

'Ken, you *can't* go out there!'

'What do we do then, stand here and watch a perfectly innocent man get killed? Betty, it's only a hundred yards or so, and if the two of us go — we're both armed.' A stray thought seemed to come to McAuliffe as he argued hardest. His words trailed off. 'I don't like the idea of leaving you here with the Olmsteads.'

Betty, knowing nothing of their suspicions, said crossly, 'Never mind the Olmsteads; she's half drunk and he's — well — I think he's a coward. The point is you have no right to risk your life like this, Mackenzie.'

Ralph moved away from them looking both anxious and impatient. Mackenzie detached himself from his wife and followed along. Betty, in the rear with her candle, continued to plead.

In the living-room, Olmstead asked what had happened outside. Ralph said tersely a tree had fallen, had struck the house in falling and that if there was damage it was not possible to detect it yet. Then he said, 'Mackenzie and I have to go out.'

Mary-Katherine, sitting impassively looked up quickly. 'Out?' she asked. 'Out there in the darkness?'

'The butler's up,' Ralph explained. 'I can't telephone to tell him to stay inside and damned if I'll cringe in here letting him walk into a bullet, or perhaps get his skull split by some damned maniac.'

As he talked, Ralph lifted the long-barrelled pistol from the waistband of his trousers, looked closely at it and shoved it back again. He looked around. Betty was ignoring them all and concentrating upon her husband, her thin, plain face grey and fear-etched. Mackenzie was in a quandary, but when Ralph started towards the dining-room, and beyond that the kitchen, Mackenzie turned and smiled at his wife.

'Nothing will happen to us, Betty. Ralph knows the grounds and we'll make it because we'll be expecting something.'

Emilio got unsteadily to his feet. 'I'll go,' he said, but even Betty McAuliffe ignored that. It was doubtful that Calderon could even get out into the kitchen, let alone across that storm-racked yard where the wind was furiously blowing again. But Calderon persisted. By utilising pieces of furniture he got several yards from his sofa. Then Mackenzie, still looking directly at this wife, said, 'Betty, look after him until we get back, will you?'

She woodenly nodded. 'Yes, of course. And you be careful out there.'

Mackenzie hastened from the room, half expecting Ralph to already be outside, but he wasn't. In the kitchen he was pulling on some rain-trousers. There was a black raincoat too. Mackenzie asked if there was another suit and Ralph pointed towards a small closet.

While they were getting rigged out Ralph said, 'Mackenzie; I wish Olmstead would come along.'

McAuliffe had a pungent observation to make about that. 'Do you? I don't. Maybe he's not involved, but all the same

I'll feel much better without him behind me out there with a gun in his hand.'

They stood a moment in the puny light of the candle Ralph had set upon a draining-board, for all the world like black effigies of some shapeless kind, gazing out a wet window. The visibility, if anything, was even worse than it had been hours earlier when there was no promise of dawn at all.

Mackenzie, tightening the drawstring of his rain-pants, said irritably, 'When the hell *does* daylight break around here, then?'

They went out through the rear porch, Ralph unlocked the door and stepped through. At once the wind struck him, rocking him left and right, then right and left. The rain, no longer ominous by itself, was broken into millions of tiny spear-heads that stung the flesh and beat against the body with infinitesimal fury. Mackenzie, catching his breath, swore heartily. Then they moved down around that pile of logs next to the door and, keeping close to the wet, clammy back-wall, got all the way to the northern corner of the house, half-protected, before the full force of the wind could even find them.

Ralph was demonstrating something he'd inherited from his father — a quiet aggressiveness and capability. He'd never done anything quite like this before yet he was assuming the initiative. Few people had equalled what he and Mackenzie were doing, and yet in every small group there was always one who'd had some variety of commando training in the armed services. Mackenzie'd had it, so possibly he was better qualified than Ralph to do the thinking for them both. But Mackenzie made no attempt to usurp Ralph's leadership.

It may not have occurred to him, or he may have been satisfied, but whatever the reason Mackenzie seemed content to follow, not lead. As long as Ralph didn't do something utterly senseless, Mackenzie probably wouldn't even offer suggestions.

One reason was undoubtedly the discomfort of being out there at all. Another reason had to be a sense of urgency both men, not so much towards Dubois, whose light was their lodestone, felt about their mission and their goal. If they could reach the staff quarters with nothing more to contend with than the wild, stormy night, it would be a blessing in disguise.

Ralph pushed off the back of the house. Behind them were those massive glass windows of the sunroom. There was something inside that seemed ghostly pale and shimmering. Someone, probably Betty, was in there with a solitary candle. Her vigil would be pointless for even if the two men weren't dressed in black on a moonless, starless night, the lack of her own light to reach past the windows would have prevented her from seeing them.

In the area between the main house and the help-house the wind caught them easily. It had force enough, but that wasn't the main problem, for as they progressed over the open ground it would hit them from behind one moment, from the left side, then from the right side, the next moment. They could never anticipate, and therefore get braced.

Also, they weren't paying as much attention to the wind as they were to the night around them.

It was useless to try and detect movement because everything that wasn't absolutely rigid, was moving, trees, bushes, plants, weeds. And along with poor visibility it was unlikely they could discern man-shapes anyway, unless they met them head-on.

There was one reasonable certainty, however: Dubois's light would, after having been detected, draw the mysterious pair of murderers. If Ralph hadn't thought that he'd never have gone out there. Of course, with two sets of armed men converging on the light in the wild darkness, enemies to say the least, the closer at least two of them got, the more wary they acted.

It was difficult to breathe despite all that fresh, wild air. Ralph developed a means for getting air by lowering his head so wind wouldn't strike him in the face. Mackenzie, six or eight feet behind, used a storm-tactic Ralph knew nothing about; he tied a handkerchief over the lower portion of his face.

Rain hit them too. It wasn't a furiously driving force the way it had once been, but with wind pushing it each tiny drop stung and was bitterly cold.

They weren't very far from the staff quarters once they'd got two-thirds of the way across the intervening distance. That light in the downstairs section looked wonderfully inviting. Dubois was doubtless in the kitchen having his first cup of coffee of the day and cursing the obligation which would impel him to leave his snug quarters.

For Mackenzie the crossing had been a nightmare only because of the storm, the abandon of the night with its noisy wind and unpleasant rain. When they had nearly completed the crossing he reached ahead to catch hold of Ralph and draw him around to signal something. Ralph put his head close.

'Gone,' yelled Mackenzie, meaning that he thought it very probable that the murderers, as he and Ralph had discussed earlier, had fled after being warned away.

Ralph looked around then bent to yell into Mackenzie's ear. 'I've been wondering . . . could they be inside?'

Mackenzie hadn't had any such thought and it shocked him. He straightened back peering towards the light up ahead. Whatever his feeling, his expression showed quick and deep-down uneasiness. Being caught out in the stormy blackness by those killers was lethal enough, but believing themselves secure and rushing into the staff quarters only to be shot down by bright light was a very unnerving prospect. He bent and said, 'Is that a lamp in there, it's awfully bright?'

'I don't know,' answered Ralph, made a grimace that was supposed to be a grin, turned and pushed on. Mackenzie noticed he was now holding that old longbarrel target pistol out in plain sight. Mackenzie reached under his own oilskins to draw forth the gun he also carried.

The manor house loomed back behind them as some great, ugly block of black that was even darker than the night. The candles back there didn't show at all, but they may not have shown in any case if everyone was in the living-room.

Ralph reached the side of the staff quarters, lay a chilled hand upon its wet-cold exterior wall and waited a moment. He and Mackenzie exchanged a squinty look, their faces drenched and pinched-looking from cold. Mackenzie gestured for Ralph to approach the house from around in back where that light shone. Ralph nodded, twisted away and started moving. The light was very bright in there; unless one knew the electricity was out in both the main house and this other place one would assume that was a hundred-watt bulb in there.

There was some shelter for the glistening, eerie, bulkily black-clad stalkers alongside the staff quarters. Bushes swinging like cat-o-nine-tails beat them unmercifully, but the same bushes also effectively camouflaged their movements.

11

To Save a Life

Dubois was indeed having his cup of coffee. When they dared look up beneath a lighted rear window and peek in, they could see him sitting there, cigarette smoking in an ashtray, the cup in his hand, hunched forward in the posture of a man entertaining some unpleasant thoughts.

Dubois's thick back and heavy shoulders were unmistakable, as were his crinkly black hair and swarthy skin. The man was one of those dark French-Canadians of whom it was often hinted the centuries-earlier conquest of Canada had left marked with an infusion of the blood of the conquered Indians.

Ralph moved down below the window, turned and beckoned to Mackenzie, then pushed and fought his way through shrubbery to the back door. There, of course, the real danger lay, for if the killers were still out there, and providing they were experienced at their business as assassins, they just might be watching that door, knowing full well that when it was opened to permit someone to pass in or out, the person would be splendidly outlined by light, an ideal target.

The alternative option was to glide around the front and seek entrance through the front door, which lay in darkness, but Ralph made no move to go in that direction. He may have been thinking that knocking on the front door couldn't be heard above the storm all the way to the back of the house, which would have been correct.

Whatever Mackenzie thought he kept to himself as he squeezed past the flourishing, tenacious limbs of a large rose-bush, complete with wicked thorns, backed against the house and turned to peer into the storm at the back.

Ralph eased closer, looked all around, then moved towards the stone steps leading to the door. Mackenzie was positioned to give him cover. Ralph looked down, saw McAuliffe facing outward, and took two large steps which placed him squarely in front of the door. He raised a wet, cold hand to fumble at the latch. It was locked from the inside, which he'd expected, but his twisting and turning alerted Dubois. In a moment the door eased inward a crack and the butler's dark features appeared in the opening. Surprised though Dubois doubtless was, he had presence enough of mind to hiss one word.

'Wait!'

The light died slowly, then the door was jerked wide enough for Ralph to squeeze through. A moment later, with scarcely any light at all, Mackenzie also got inside. Water dripped in pools all around them. The light Mackenzie had wondered about turned out to be one of those oil-burning Coleman lamps which operated by pumped-in air pressure. When properly functioning they gave off as much light as an electric bulb, except that brightness was pure white with none of the yellowish tones of an electric bulb. Also, this kind of lamp made a steady little hissing sound. If they'd had such a contrivance over at the main house the loss of electric power wouldn't have bothered them so much.

Dubois, seeing the guns, the drawn, grey faces and the dark-ringed eyes, looked amazed. 'What is it?' he whispered.

Ralph told him. 'My father was murdered last night. There are some men outside, somewhere.' Ralph moved clear of the nearest window and sought a chair, putting his back to the stone wall as he sat, dripping water and looking half dead. 'The Central American was nearly killed too. We saw your light over here and came to warn you against going outside.'

'I?' said Dubois, his black gaze fixed upon Ralph.

Mackenzie took it up. 'We don't know what they want, Dubois, but we *do* know they will attack anyone they catch outside. Mister Calderon is only a guest, but they nearly brained him when he tried to reach the cars and go for help.'

The French-Canadian went over to the table, started to resume his chair, then suddenly remembering the window, jumped away as though stung. He made a little wringing gesture with his hands, 'Why?' he asked plaintively. 'What do they want? All I know is that the lights were gone when I got up this morning, but the storm seems to be breaking up.'

'The telephone is gone too,' said Mackenzie, a bit laconically. 'Dubois, is there a gun here?'

'A gun? Well, yes, there are several rifles. I think there is a pistol too, somewhere.'

'A rifle will be cumbersome,' said McAuliffe. 'Better get the pistol, though, if you can find it.'

The butler was still having difficulty grasping all this. He stood staring at McAuliffe, his black eyes perfectly round. Finally he said, looking at Ralph, 'But the police . . . '

'They'll be here eventually,' said Ralph. 'Providing the road isn't washed out. We managed to get word out.'

Dubois was suddenly relieved. 'I'll get you some coffee,' he said, and went after cups. As he was pouring, over at the stove, he looked back at Ralph. 'Why would someone hurt your father?'

Ralph simply shook his head. All the butler's questions had rung through his own mind for so long now they seemed no longer to possess genuine significance. Reaction was setting in, for Ralph, who had made the deadly crossing and who was now slumped and bone-weary.

Dubois brought their cups and stood gazing at them. They were surrounded by puddles of water. Their rain suits had been torn in a dozen places by thorns and pointed limbs. Their faces, even though the kitchen was warm, still looked pinched with cold.

Dubois went to a cupboard, dug out a bottle of whisky and went to pour some into the cups they held out for it. He then looked at the lamp, hissing still although it had been turned so low that shadows filled the low-ceilinged kitchen.

There were two other servants, a maid and her husband. The latter took care of the grounds. Dubois mentioned them, saying they were still asleep in their upstairs room. He wondered if they shouldn't also be brought to the kitchen and told what was happening.

Ralph didn't think so and Mackenzie, feeling new, warm life spiralling outwards from his stomach as coffee and whisky took hold, kept silent on this topic.

Finally, the butler's astonishment seemed to depart; the shock was over and he was accepting the situation. He said, 'I'll see if I can find the pistol. Then we can return to the manor house. What of the other people over there?'

Ralph said in a toneless voice they were barricaded behind locked doors, and that evidently the killers had decided not to try and get inside; at least they hadn't during the worst of the storm and throughout all the worst hours of this nightmarish night.

Dubois stood irresolute, not moving, then he said, 'I think I could reach the village.'

Mackenzie at once broke in. 'I doubt that you could, but if the police are on their way, what would be the point of perhaps getting killed to do it?'

Dubois nodded thoughtfully, then said,

'But how long ago did you talk to them? It only takes a little while to drive this far.'

That, of course, was the enigma; in Ralph's mind, and Mackenzie's mind too, it seemed that ample time had passed for help to have arrived. But it *hadn't* arrived.

Dubois shrugged and reverted to his early thought. 'I'll see where the pistol is.' He left the room.

Ralph finished off his spiked coffee, leaned to set the cup on an oilcloth-covered table, then rummaged inside all his clothing for a cigarette. He lit up, looked around at the streaked window nearest him and said, 'Maybe they *did* pull out, Mackenzie.'

It was the kind of statement that could be right as rain or wrong as hell; it neither encouraged nor required comment. McAuliffe went on sipping his coffee. He was leaning upon the back-wall. After a while he said, 'Olmstead. I think when we get back the thing to do is question him. If he lies again, the way he did about signalling with that torch, we should confront him with the facts . . . Perhaps use a little coercion, Ralph. This thing is going to head-up before dawn comes — if it ever *does* come. Normally I disapprove of force, but this is different.'

He didn't say *why* it was different, but then he didn't have to exlain why that was. Death had come to Masters Manor. It could very easily come again. People in peril of being shot to death were likely to lose a good deal of their normal idealism. Evidently Mackenzie McAuliffe was such a person in such a situation.

Ralph said nothing. He was reacting to the stillness and warmth of the room, which permeated each muscle and nerve making him gradually loosen on his chair feeling as though he could pass the balance of his life in this delicious limbo.

It was his conscience that finally made him say, 'All right. Olmstead knows *something*, I'm convinced of that. I suppose we should have leaned on him a long time ago.'

Mackenzie's thoughts had already left

the subject of Frank Olmstead and were dwelling upon what was infinitely closer to him. 'What a hell of a nightmare this has been for Betty. She's alone over there with those two.' He obviously meant the Olmsteads but whether he'd have explained that or not, probably not, he didn't get the chance because Dubois returned with a heavy, ugly, badly-balanced and poorly engineered big old U.S. Army .45 calibre automatic in one hand. The gun was too heavy, too cumbersome, and too treacherous to be trusted even by the man standing behind it, but it was a weapon, and its bullet, at a reasonable distance, was very deadly.

The gun showed dust and oil but it had no visible, external rust showing. Dubois silently slipped out the clip to show that the gun was loaded to capacity. As he knocked the clip back up the handle he said, 'It was in an old foot-locker. I thought that was where I'd seen it one time.' He looked without any affection at the big pistol. 'I have never fired one of these. They say the recoil is bad and that they jam easily.

Well, it is this thing or a rifle.' Dubois shrugged and pushed the weapon under his jacket. He had also, while he was out of the room, donned a raincoat that reached to his ankles. It was black and dusty and made the butler took like an undertaker. He didn't have the build for wearing any kind of coat really, being short, squat and bear-like.

Evidently, during his absence, Dubois had been doing some thinking, because he turned to Ralph and said, 'If those men are burglars they won't still be out there, will they? What would be their point, if they knew they'd been discovered? Besides, it is a very bad night for remaining out of doors,'

'They're not burglars,' Ralph asserted getting heavily to his feet. 'Dubois, when we go outside, stay close and keep watching for anything that resembles a man. Shoot if you see something.'

'Anything, Mister Fielding? But suppose the police are out there.'

'Shoot,' repeated Ralph grimly. 'If the police are out there we'll know it because they'll have lights on their cars. But they *won't* be out there.' Ralph didn't explain that last sentence until he got to the door and motioned for someone to kill the light entirely. Then he said, 'Look over at the main house. If the police had arrived there'd be lights over there. Lamps or torches. It's as dark as ever. Okay, Dubois, kill the light and let's go.'

The butler twisted that small copper handle that permitted air to reach the lamp mantles and the glow died slowly. None of them moved until all the light was gone, then Ralph opened the door, stood beside it a moment bracing into the wind-driven rain straining to see out. Mackenzie and Dubois edged up behind him. The two taller men knew what had to be done to get back across the wild distance, they also knew what course to follow — the same one they'd used reaching the staff quarters. Also, they were fresh again, thanks to black coffee laced with whisky.

Ralph stepped out, glided to the left and dropped instantly down among the flowers and bushes alongside the house.

Mackenzie came next and finally Dubois slid round the door and dropped into the muddy, cold darkness with wind tearing the breath from his nostrils.

Again Ralph led out. He followed his exact steps as far as the corner of the staff quarters. There, when the other two crowded him he turned, having an errant thought, pushed his face to Dubois's ear and said, 'Did you — tell the maid and her husband — not to leave the staff quarters?'

Dubois nodded.

Mackenzie nudged Ralph and pointed. Off to their right and somewhere between the staff quarters and the main mansion, a wet light flickered on briefly, then flickered out. It had been directed in their area, as though someone might be out a little distance away closing in on the staff quarters.

Mackenzie called Olmstead's name aloud and added a savage epithet to it. 'Of course,' he said. 'He'd signal about us being out here, wouldn't he?'

12

Blood and Mud

The worst feature of death, obviously, is anticipating it. Whoever saw a person, brought to death's door, who wasn't relaxed and limp?

It was this anticipation that made the three men beside the stone staff quarters stiffen instantly, and remain alert after that brief, weak glow had come and gone. Ralph, setting a course, moved away from their shelter and the wind hit them hard, but there was no longer any water in it. Evidently, while he and Mackenzie had been inside, the rain had gone.

The wind was still damp and uncomfortably cold and it still possessed its buffeting force as the three of them dropped eastward, down towards the front of the staff quarters, which was away from their former route. Ralph was clearly adopting the instinctive ruse of trapped people; he was seeking to trade space for time. While those stalking killers closed in on the staff quarters, he was offering them all the area around it, uninhabited and abandoned.

The trouble with such strategy was that since it was as old as the first manhunt, the hunters were just as possibly aware of its possibilities as were the hunted.

Mackenzie, who'd had a little training in matters of this kind, hardly enough to classify him as a professional but certainly more than Ralph, and apparently Dubois either, had had, halted his companions a hundred feet below the staff quarters, motioned for them to squat down, then did what he hadn't attempted earlier; assumed some of the command of their little expedition by saying through cupped hands that their stalkers would assuredly split up and try to catch them midway.

Dubois nodded and Ralph waited motionless for whatever this statement was the prelude for. It was a short wait. Mackenzie said, 'We go back.'

Dubois looked up quickly. Ralph stared too. Mackenzie didn't have to elaborate, he meant they should turn from hunted to hunters. He added the key word to that suggestion.

'Ambush.'

Dubois looked at the big pistol he had and looked around through the darkness. Suddenly he made a low grunt and jutted his jaw towards the gusty east. There was a razor-thin streak of wet blue paleness over there. Dawn was coming. There was no other light though, which probably meant that even when dawn finally arrived daylight wasn't going to be any sunburst of warmth and singing birds and delight. The storm had passed, obviously. They'd had no lightning nor thunder for many hours, and even the rain was finally gone too, but the wind, the low scudding sooty clouds, the rawness, remained to either presage a new storm or to sullenly signify the reluctant withdrawal of the former storm.

'Light won't be in our favour,' said Mackenzie, twisting to look back towards the staff quarters, any more than it will be in *their* favour. We've got to be out of here before it comes.'

'Then we'd better keep moving towards the manor,' said Ralph.

Dubois spoke. 'One should be behind us by now. The other one . . . ' Dubois peered ahead towards the main house and eloquently shrugged, meaning the other one was probably down there somewhere waiting.

'That's what they're expecting,' Mackenzie told Ralph. 'Come along.' He didn't offer any additional argument, but turned and began retracing his steps towards the staff quarters. It was the wrong direction of course, and even granting they were fortunate enough to fulfil Mackenzie's wish — knocking out one of the assassins — they'd still have to turn about eventually, try to reach the main house, and that other assassin would probably still be lying in wait for them. Only now there was that thin sliver of light off in the east. If it kept widening it was ultimately going to betray them as they tried getting across the intervening distance between both buildings.

The problem was one of those dilemmas that seemed to endlessly compound itself. Still, Mackenzie, taking over full leadership now, moved resolutely back towards the front of the staff quarters, and meanwhile the wind rose a notch or two, hammering them almost flat at times, then sucking back to leave them crouched and braced, in a temporary hushed vacuum while it struck at one of the stone houses, or went swooping off into the distant forest where it made hideous screams which carried easily down to where the men were.

When the confrontation arrived it came so suddenly no one was prepared for it even though each of them was alert and tensed for trouble. A flat sound spanked the night off to their left, midway between them and the rear of the staff quarters. Wind picked up that sound and whipped it away, but the way Dubois dropped was unmistakable to Ralph, who was slightly to his right and behind him.

Mackenzie answered that gunflash and Ralph, who hadn't seen it, spurted ahead to Dubois. The French-Canadian looked up at him from wide-open eyes, too stunned evidently to comprehend at once that he'd been hit. Ralph found the wound, which explained some of the butler's rigid shock. There was a four-inch furrow alongside Dubois's head where scalp and hair had been cut away as neatly as though accomplished by a surgeon's scalpel. The wonder was that the French-Canadian was able to look up at all. He should be all rights have been unconscious, if not from shock, then perhaps from the wound itself which was bleeding profusely and looked deep enough to have left a thin strip of skull exposed. Apparently Dubois was blessed with an inordinately thick skull.

Another of those flat, spanking reports came. This time both Ralph and Mackenzie saw it. This time too, Ralph lifted the long-barrelled target-pistol, aimed left and fired, aimed right and fired, aimed dead-centre and fired.

Mackenzie got off two rounds.

An odd thing occurred. The next tearing and jagged burst of gun-flame was directed straight down. It was visible to both Mackenzie and Ralph Fielding. Mackenzie said something loudly but the wind whipped it away and Ralph turned back to find a handkerchief to push against Dubois's head to stop the blood from flowing. Mackenzie leaned to help. Between them they got Dubois bandaged. The bleeding was suppressed but not halted by any means; Dubois's bandage turned stickily scarlet at once, which may not have been entirely detrimental since the handkerchief, being white, would have advertised his whereabouts.

They told him to lie perfectly still and keep watch. Whether he understood that order or not was problematical although he looked squarely at them when it was said, then Mackenzie and Ralph went crawling with extreme caution up towards that black patch they'd fired at.

They found the man. He was dead and without an externally visible mark on him, but then he was clothed in black oilskins exactly as they were, but with a heavy wool sweater beneath the coat. He'd also had a rain cap, complete with tip-down visor, but that lay in the mud now and his close-cropped hair, like his upturned face, was full of wet mud.

Mackenzie said, 'Do you know him?'

Ralph looked closely. 'No. He's not a local man.' He picked up the gun half buried in mud at the man's side. 'Luger,' he said. 'German Luger.' Mackenzie looked, nodded indifferently, and knelt over to wrench at the oilskin fastenings. He plunged both hands inside the man's sweater, into one pocket after another until he'd taken everything he found except some money that he let fall into the mud, then he jerked his head and started back towards Dubois.

The butler's trauma was passing. He was holding his head in both hands, the .45 pistol lying in his lap. The sight of so much blood most of it water-diluted but still a disconcerting amount in any event, had shaken Dubois badly. When the other two got back to him he said something in *patois* that might have been indistinguishable even without the wind to distort it, and rocked back and forth still holding his head.

Ralph dropped a hand upon the butler's shoulder. 'You're lucky,' he called through the wind. 'At least *you're* alive.' His emphasis brought the French-Canadian's head up.

'You got that one?' he asked.

Ralph and Mackenzie nodded, then they helped him to his feet, kept him between them and started eastward, directly away from both the staff quarters and the mansion. By unspoken accord they set an entirely different course from the earlier route. Now, they were going towards the distant roadway, and not towards the manor house at all.

It seemed a good choice but even so, after a bit, when Dubois seemed able to navigate by himself, a little wobbly but still without falling, Mackenzie made a hand-motion that Ralph could understand, and went ahead to reconnoitre.

Ralph kept moving, but more slowly, and with one eye on the unsteady butler who looked a frightfully gory mess even without anything better than blackness to see him by.

If the surviving assassin had heard or seen the flashes of that furious, brief gun-battle back there, which was very probable, by now he might also have located his dead friend. If this were so, even if he burned with a desire for vengeance, it seemed very unlikely that he'd come charging down at them, and even less likely that he'd guess they'd changed course and weren't moving towards the safety of the manor house at all.

Ralph kept close watch on both sides and behind them even though he did not anticipate another brush with their unknown enemy. He was quite satisfied, the way Mackenzie's ambush scheme had worked out, since Dubois hadn't been killed, as he'd initially thought had been the case.

When Dubois's legs became more unsteady than ever, Ralph eased him down near a great old fir tree whose needles, green though they were, had been nearly all stripped from the outermost branches, carpeting the mud for acres in all directions. He then started out to locate McAuliffe.

By looking over his right shoulder, Ralph had the entire front of the manor house in sight. There was a feeble glow coming past the front windows, and a great, but redder glow — the fireplace no doubt — flickering brighter, then darker, then brighter again.

McAuliffe stepped out of the blackness, caught Ralph's eye instantly, and came forward shaking his head. He had seen nor heard nothing that alerted him. He proposed that they bring Dubois along and try to enter the house from the front door. He also said, whether the surviving assassin had found his companion yet or not, by now he'd know by his inability to contact him, there was plenty of reason to be extremely careful, and therefore might be content to withdraw and hide rather than try another ambush along the front of the house.

They went back for the butler, got him to his feet and started for the front of the house. Now, thick skull notwithstanding, Dubois complained of a roaring headache. It would have been totally unbelievable if he hadn't complained of one.

Reaching the house was complicated by fresh bursts of wind which tore at them, and also by Dubois's delayed reaction, which finally set in causing the French-Canadian to falter and nearly fall several times. Ralph was on one side, Mackenzie on the other side. They each had their free hand beneath the butler's arm, assisting him, guns naked in their other hands.

The distance was great but they halted twice to catch their breath. It was like swimming against a powerful tide — with a weight tied to one's ankles.

This was when they were most vulnerable, and both of them knew it. Each time they halted to catch their breath they looked very carefully all around.

But the surviving killer evidently was no longer seeking a fight, or, if he was, he hadn't thought his prey would be coming up towards the house from the direction of the distant road.

They reached the recessed doorway, pushed Dubois in out of the wind, then rested a moment, themselves protected by the large opening in the stone wall.

Ralph said, 'What was in his pockets?'

referring to whatever it was Mackenzie had taken from the corpse. The answer he got back wasn't very enlightening.

'I didn't look. We'll be able to inside. One thing he had . . . ' Mackenzie fished forth a small black booklet and help it up. 'Unless it's something else I'd say it must be an address-book or a diary. I'd settle for either one of them.'

He shoved the book back under his oilskins and jerked his head for Ralph to beat on the massive oaken door. Ralph obliged by using the butt of his target-pistol, quite oblivious to the squawks of startled consternation this ominous sound made inside the living-room where it echoed round the room like the blows of an axe.

13

An Exasperating Experience

Betty McAuliffe was so pleased at the return of her husband she clung to him in spite of the frightful sight his companion, the wounded butler, presented, They had heard some gunshots. Mary-Katherine Olmstead, sober or very nearly so, and Frank Olmstead, helped Dubois to a chair. Emilio Calderon had already gone for coffee. He was continuing his remarkable recovery. Mary-Katherine had helped Betty change Emilio's bandage, make it smaller, so although he was purple below both eyes and there was extensive swelling, Emilio looked much better.

If one compared him to Dubois he looked incomparably better, for Dubois had splashed blood down the front and right side of his oilskins. It had even managed to trickle beneath on to his other clothing. His head was rapidly swelling. Betty, gently removing Dubois's improvised and cumbersome bandage, looked closely at his wound and said it should be stitched before the swelling made this impossible.

No one had any suggestions or comments to make about that. There were no doctors among them.

They made Dubois as comfortable as they could on the same couch Calderon had used, covered him with blankets and got some laced coffee down him. He was feeling very ill by that time, and of course the wonder was that he had not collapsed long before.

Olmstead said, 'Well, you saved his bacon, but in the process damned near got him killed.'

Neither Mackenzie nor Ralph looked at the older man when he said this, nor made any comment. Betty and Emilio wanted to know about the gunshots they'd heard. Mackenzie smiled at them, withdrew the objects from his pocket he'd taken from the slain stranger, carefully arranged them upon a table in plain sight, and looked steadily at Frank Olmstead as he said, 'Did you all stay here by the fireplace while we were out there?'

Betty answered, saying she'd gone to the sunroom several times trying to see out. Mary-Katherine said she'd gone upstairs to get an aspirin. Frank Olmstead said he'd gone upstairs to bring his wife back down; he didn't like the idea of her being up there alone. He might have added that he suspected she had a bottle hidden up there, which would have sounded believable, but he didn't.

Ralph, looking at the objects Mackenzie had put upon the table, picked up the little black book. On the first page in a laborious scrawl was written directions for reaching Brentsboro, and on the adjoining page was a crude map for reaching Masters Manor from the village. On the next page were some figures someone had added up. They could have been mileage or they could have been sums of money, there was no explanation. Otherwise, the little book had no writing in it. Ralph handed the thing to Mackenzie who stood silently studying it for a moment.

Olmstead came over to examine the other effects. There was a small pencil-flashlight that worked when Olmstead tested it, a large switchblade knife — illegal to carry, but then that wouldn't have deterred a man who was by trade an assassin — and there was a wallet. This latter object proved the most rewarding. Apart from a fat packet of money there were several credit cards — all made out to different names — plus two letters, both beginning with 'Dear Mike.' One of the names on the credit cards was Michael King. A newspaper clipping carefully folded and showing evidence of age, told the story of a hijacked coastal steamer named the *Princess of Porto Bello*. The only name listed in the story was of the ship's captain, one Angelo Bordhese. The ship had been carrying a cargo of dried fish; it was in fact a small coastal vessel that plied the waters between several small Italian towns, and there was a hint to the dispatch indicating that the *Princess of Porto Bello* might have been carrying some kind of contraband, although evidently this was not known to be true at the time the article was printed because the hint was carefully worded.

The letters were both in Italian, which no one could read although Ralph Fielding took one letter over to the fireplace to mull over. He told Betty McAuliffe that he'd taken French in college, which enabled him to pick out a word here and there.

It was Emilio Calderon, glancing through the other letter, who came closest to interpreting the words. He said, 'I think your dead man's name was Reino or something like that, which would in fact be translatable in English to something like King. But otherwise this letter is from some woman who longs to have him return to her. She lives in New York. She signs only her first name, Gina, which isn't a proper name at all, but is rather a diminutive.' Emilio shrugged. Her real name could be one of several. Emilio put down his letter and went over to examine the one Ralph was struggling with.

But the second letter was even more

obscure. It was from a man and it was unsigned. The wording was different, the handwriting stronger and heavier. Its substance, Emilio thought, dealt with someone's share of something that hadn't been delivered. There was an underlying sense of indignation to this letter. At least it seemed that way to Emilio, but even as he said this he also said he wasn't quite sure, that his knowledge of Italian, while it helped, was not likely to allow him to pick out the actual nuances.

Frank Olmstead, examining the wallet, turned and said, 'Okay, so his name was King. What else?' Olmstead gestured with contempt towards the black book, the knife, the wallet. 'There's not enough here to tell us anything.'

Ralph gazed at the large, older man, from quiet, speculative eyes. Mackenzie, in the act of stripping off his punctured, soiled oilskins, paused long enough to light a cigarette and also gaze a moment at Olmstead. He too was silent.

It was undoubtedly the attitude of these two that contributed mostly to the odd, noticeable tension, that came into the room now. Finally, replacing the letter on the table holding the dead assassin's other things, Ralph said, 'Olmstead, where is your flashlight?'

The older man looked steadily at Fielding without answering for a long moment. The others, excepting Dubois who was lying on the sofa in pain, looked quickly at Ralph, whose tone hadn't been at all congenial.

Olmstead finally said, 'What flashlight, Fielding? What are you trying to say?'

Ralph moved a little closer to the older man. 'The flashlight you used to signal from the upstairs window with.'

Olmstead kept staring at Fielding. Evidently he was a man of swift perception, which was plausible since he happened to also be a highly successful international businessman. He slowly moved clear of the table and swung his head to include Mckenzie McAuliffe in his stare. Then he said, 'Let's have it you two. What's this all about?'

'A lie you told will do for openers,' said Ralph.

Olmstead again wore the expression of

a man who knew something in advance. He said, 'Out with it.'

Emilio, Betty McAuliffe, Mary-Katherine, were like statues, watching and listening. The only person, in fact, who moved even slightly, was Frank Olmstead. He seemed less tense than anyone else whether his back was to the wall or not.

'You said you didn't leave the kitchen when you and your wife went out there to make coffee. That was a lie, Olmstead. I went out for logs to put in the fireplace and neither of you were there. Later, when I asked about you leaving the room, you said you hadn't.'

Ralph and Mackenzie were watching Olmstead very closely now, as though they expected him to do something desperate. He acted as though nothing was further from his mind. He even smiled slightly, the way a parent might smile at an annoying child.

'Very clever,' he said to Ralph, being heavily sarcastic. 'Okay, Mary-Katherine had to go upstairs. If I have to spell it out for you — there was no bathroom in the kitchen. I stayed in the kitchen, then I got uneasy, the same as either one of you would have; after all this is a murder-maze of a house. I didn't want her up there alone so I went to make certain she was all right. I was out of the kitchen maybe five, maybe ten minutes. That didn't constitute much of a departure did it? Or do you think someone opened the back door and let a horde of monkeys into the house?'

With enormous disgust Olmstead walked across to the fireplace, turned his back to the flames and surveyed his interrogators. Then gave his head a big negative shake.

'This is the most outlandish situation I've ever been in. And believe me, in my travels round the world I've been in some dillies. Moreover, by your own admission, Ralph, and the admission of your father, you've had some genuine lunatics in your family. I have no explanation for the killing of Hugh, and although neither you nor McAuliffe will believe it, evidently, I have no explanation for those two men sneaking around outside in the storm wanting to keep us bottled up in here, or kill us. But I don't give a damn what either of you pups think, so do whatever you've a mind to.'

'Tell me you didn't signal with a flashlight from McAuliffe's bedroom window,' exclaimed Ralph.

Olmstead remained obdurate on that point. 'I didn't signal anyone from any bedroom window. You asked, and I've just told you.'

Mackenzie said softly, 'Another lie, Mister Olmstead?'

Finally, the big, older man's patience slipped. He turned on McAuliffe who was some distance away, as though he might hurl himself forward. His reply was delayed a moment, but eventually he said, 'McAuliffe, I've never taken being called a liar from anyone, but twice within the last few minutes I've let it go. Let me tell you something: I don't have to lie to you or to anyone else. I can buy you and sell you out of my watch-pocket. Do you imagine for a moment if I was behind all this mess I'd commit either myself or my wife to the same danger? And one more thing,

McAuliffe — call me a liar one more time and I'll knock your head off!'

The silence was thick enough to cut with a knife after Olmstead stopped speaking. Calderon was the first to move, finally; he went to Dubois with some whisky and a damp, cool rag. That gave a cue to the women; Betty went over by her husband, who was putting out a cigarette, and stole her fingers into his hand. He squeezed and smiled at her.

Ralph alone among them was not ready to admit there was a stalemate. 'What was your purpose in coming here?' he asked Olmstead. 'I know — my father invited you. But why?'

'If I thought it was any of your business,' replied the harassed older man, 'I'd tell you.'

'It's my business now,' retorted Ralph sharply, anger clearly showing in his face.

'If you mean because Hugh is dead, I differ about that. You may be his heir, Ralph, but the courts will decide what you inherit.' Olmstead stood a moment looking into the younger man's angry countenance, then he suddenly said, 'All right. I'll tell you why my wife and I came to this rock-pile. Because your father and I were about to form a company to handle the promotional end of a piece of ocean frontage I acquired last year in Europe. Originally, I wanted him simply to arrange the advertising campaign. Then he wanted a piece of the action, so in lieu of payment for his work, I'd been discussing this separate company with him. He invited me down a week ago so we could possibly finalise things. That's why I'm here. And I wish to God I'd never even come near Masters Manor.' The way Olmstead said the name of the Fielding mansion made it sound dirty.

Ralph flushed and turned as Dubois groaned. Emilio was propping him up with pillows. Evidently even that slight movement had caused additional pain.

Mary-Katherine said brightly, 'What we all need is a drink,' and turned towards the bar. Her husband intercepted her, and this time, ignoring the on-lookers, caught her arm, twisted it behind her back, turned her back and gave her a rough push towards a chair. 'Sit down,' he grated. 'Dammit, I've had about enough — from *all* of you!'

Finally, Frank Olmstead was ready to let himself go. The look, the stance, the deepening colour, all were unmistakable evidence of his fighting frame of mind.

McAuliffe did an odd thing. He strolled over to the bar, mixed a drink, brought it back and handed it to Olmstead.

'Take it easy,' he said quietly. 'Pretty bad night for nerves.' He then went over to pick up the soggy oilskins he'd dropped and strode past Ralph towards the kitchen with them in his hands without even looking at Fielding.

14

A Glimmer of Hope

Something had definitely gone very wrong. Ralph followed Mackenzie out into the kitchen. Shortly after he entered, so did Betty. Ralph said, 'Mackenzie, you believed him,' making it sound like an accusation.

McAuliffe deposited the oilskins on the back-porch, came into the doorway and looking straight at Ralph said, 'I wish to hell I knew whether I believed the man or not, Ralph.' McAuliffe's voice dragged with tiredness. 'His answers made sense.'

'He's quick-witted,' retorted Ralph. 'You ought to have observed that by now. He's damned clever.'

Betty broke in. 'He was concerned when you two were out there, Ralph. He took a gun and stood by a window when we heard those shots. He was ready to help you.'

‘Or help the man we killed,’ said Ralph, and sank down upon a kitchen chair to remove the oilskins he was still wearing. ‘I wish to hell that stuff we got off the dead man told us more.’

McAuliffe lit a cigarette, exhaled a gust of grey smoke and said, ‘All we’ve got to do now is wait. It’ll be daylight shortly, and the police will surely get here by then.’

Betty looked from Ralph to her husband. ‘I think Dubois has a mild concussion, Ken,’ she said softly. ‘He’s turning black-and-blue all down that side of his face and his eyes don’t quite focus.’

‘He’ll make it,’ replied her husband. ‘If he’s got this far he’ll make it, love. And there’s nothing we can do anyway, until help arrives.’

The kitchen door swung open. Emilio stood in the opening. ‘Maybe we could make something to eat,’ he said, and smiled at them all.

Betty responded to this pleasant change by nodding and going towards a cupboard. Ralph kicked aside his discarded oilskins and blew out a big, unsteady sigh. 'If my father had only *said* something,' he muttered, and turned to leave the room. Ralph followed along leaving his wife and Calderon in the kitchen.

Mary-Katherine was glaring venomously at her husband. Evidently they'd had another of their savage, swift arguments during the absence of the others. Now, though, there were only the sulphurous glares back and forth to indicate this might be so.

No one spoke. Ralph dropped into a chair near the fireplace looking moodily at the back of the sofa where the butler lay. Mackenzie got himself a glass of beer from the bar, and that seemed to inspire Olmstead to do the same.

Olmstead ignored Ralph completely, his animus still evident when he glanced in the younger man's direction, and took a position by the fireplace not far from Mackenzie as he said, watching the foam on the beer glass in his hand, 'The other one probably has left by now. He'd probably think he was on the short end, with four or five armed men in the house, and he being all alone out there now.'

Mackenzie glanced up, waiting. Olmstead met his look with a hard glance.

'Maybe I could get one of the cars started.'

Mary-Katherine said bitterly, 'You? A mechanic? Frank, you even have trouble making your cigarette lighter work properly.'

Olmstead ignored that although a faint blush appeared in his cheeks, barely noticeable in the poor light of the room. He kept looking at McAuliffe, finally lifting his lips in a rueful, mirthless little smile.

'Okay. That's true enough. But if they did something simple like yanking off battery cables, maybe I could fix it.'

Mackenzie sipped his beer in quiet thought, and slid a glance in Ralph's direction before he said, 'It's an idea. Maybe that other gunman *has* fled by now. Ralph . . . ?'

'What?'

'The three of us can go see about the cars.'

Fielding looked up, shot a glance at Olmstead, then looked steadily at McAuliffe for a moment as though reaching for whatever was in the other man's mind. Finally, he nodded and rose. He still had the target-pistol stuffed into the waistband of his trousers but he'd placed the Luger, removed from the dead assassin, over on that little table with the dead man's other possessions.

He looked squarely at Olmstead. 'If you have anything else in mind,' he said softly, 'forget it.'

Olmstead whirled but McAuliffe was on his feet in smooth, swift motion. 'Let's just concentrate on this other thing for a while,' he barked, stepping between Fielding and Olmstead. 'Better get your coats, it's cold out there.'

They told Mary-Katherine to lock the front door after them and Olmstead, staring at his wife, shook his head ever so slightly at her. 'No more,' he said, the meaning very clear. 'Go help in the kitchen if you like, but don't go near that bar again.'

The door closed angrily behind them

and Olmstead, who hadn't been out before, reached up to button the jacket he wore.

It *was* cold out, exactly as McAuliffe had said it would be. Also, the wind, though still blowing, seemed to have risen to about rooftop-height. It buffeted them as they left the recessed front entrance-way, but not nearly as bitterly as it had hit people an hour or more before.

The sky too seemed higher, and there were rents in it as though the higher pinnacles of that furious wind up there were tearing it apart. Off in the east that knife-edged long sliver of sickly blue light was wider by perhaps a yard or two, but darkness still reigned even though, under normal weather conditions, by now daylight should have been close.

They stopped a moment to look off in the direction of the roadway. Olmstead said bitterly that any other place on earth the damned police would have arrived by now. Then he stepped out with a thrusting stride heading towards the area beside the house where a *porte-cochere*, erected centuries later, shielded four of the cars, but left two unsheltered.

They went for the car nearest them beneath the *porte-cochere*. It was Olmstead's tank-like over-large and massive, baby-blue Cadillac four-door. Its owner slid under the wheel and pumped the gas-pedal before switching on the key, which also activated the starting motor. The heavy motor revved up encouragingly, but did not catch hold. Olmstead swore fiercely and repeated the process but his Cadillac did not start. He looked out, pulled a handle beneath the dashboard, then heaved around and alighted, went up front and raised the hood. Mackenzie reached inside, located the light-switch and pulled it. Nothing happened, and of course that was a clue; if there was no electricity reaching the lights, yet the starter worked indicating that current was still passing out of the battery, it was highly probable that someone had reached beneath the dashboard to tear loose some wires.

Mackenzie got down low and held his cigarette lighter up until he could see beneath the dashboard. He grunted, crawled out and said, 'Forget it, Olmstead. About half your ignition wires have been torn out. It'd take two hours to get this car running.'

They went to the next car, which was Calderon's sleek, low-slung Jaguar, pale cream in colour with dark red upholstery. Here they were more successful, the motor ran up on its windings, then coughed and took hold. Olmstead smiled, the first such expression he'd showed that reflected real pleasure.

'Climb out,' he said to Ralph, who had started the car. 'Stay with the women. This shouldn't take long. The village is only a mile or two down the road, isn't it?'

Ralph sat still, gazing at the older man without making any move to relinquish the seat. He pressed on the accelerator several times to keep the motor alive. Mackenzie, standing beside Olmstead, frowned slightly. He may or he may not, have guessed what was passing through Fielding's mind, but his expression indicated fresh exasperation, and before anything more could be said, he rapped out what was in his own mind.

'Damn it, like my wife said, just for a little longer can't we try to get along?'

Ralph spoke, still from the seat of Calderon's car. 'And suppose Mister Olmstead just keeps right on going, Mackenzie? What's to prevent it?'

Olmstead, finally comprehending that look on Ralph's face, rolled big hands up into big fists. His smile was gone in a second and the leashed fury was up again.

But it was McAuliffe who once more got between them. '*You* go,' he said to Ralph. To Olmstead he said, 'He knows the road anyway. If there's a washout or something he'd know how to get around or over it. You'll go back inside with me.'

Olmstead said thinly, 'Is that an order, McAuliffe?'

Mackenzie shook his head wearily. 'No, it's not an order. It's just a suggestion. If you prefer, we can sit out here and freeze until he gets back.'

'You're with him in believing those

ridiculous accusations, though, aren't you?'

Again McAuliffe shook his head. 'To tell you the truth. I'm not very sure what I believe, Olmstead, except that one man is dead and two more damned near got killed.' McAuliffe turned. 'Go on, Ralph. There's got to be something seriously wrong down the line or the police would have been here by now. You've got to make it though.'

Ralph nodded, closed the door, eased the car into reverse and backed clear. As he made the full swing into the driveway he turned on the headlights and a great are of light swung all along the front of the house. There was nothing there but broken and battered shrubbery and the pale, puny candle-light coming from the front windows.

As they stood watching Ralph drive off, Frank Olmstead said, 'You're right, we've got to hang together a bit longer. Although that damned pup has been rubbing me the wrong way all night.'

Mackenzie, watching the scarlet tail-lamps cruise down to the gateway, then swing left, sighed and said, 'In his boots, with your father dead inside, how would you have reacted?'

'Okay,' grumbled the internationalist. 'It didn't come to anything. It came close, but it didn't come to anything.' Olmstead's eyes swung to consider McAuliffe. 'You've been on my back too, McAuliffe.'

Mackenzie made no attempt to deny it. He said, 'Nerves, anxiety, bewilderment, I guess.' He slowly met the older man's stare. 'Someone of us is involved, I'm convinced of that.'

Olmstead's lips flattened and dropped as he sarcastically said, 'Why does that have to be so? Because you can't imagine these damned Fieldings having local enemies? Hell's bells, McAuliffe, you heard about the pair of nuts who hanged their own son and brother. And about that other one that refused to meet his income-tax obligation; and now this insane business of a nightmare in their thirty-room pile of fieldstone. If you were to ask me I'd say Hugh and his son are capable of having done something to the people in their village that would have caused all this business. And I'll tell you something else too: the quicker I can get out of here and see the last of this whole lunatic asylum the happier I'll be!'

Mackenzie could agree with the last part of all this, if not necessarily with the first part. He looked around, saw nothing that interested him, pushed cold hands into trouser pockets and suggested they go back inside by the fire.

Olmstead grunted assent and struck out with that same thrusting stride again, heading back the way he'd come. At the doorway he looked along the front of the house, up at the shredding sky, down where the Jaguar's tail-lamps had disappeared, and swore with hearty feeling. He didn't have to say what his mood was, nor what his thoughts were. Monumental disgust.

McAuliffe's private reflections were that either Olmstead was as innocent of complicity as he said, or he was one of the best actors Mackenzie had ever encountered.

They entered the house when Betty answered Olmstead's furious pounding on the door, closed, locked the door behind them, and Olmstead, looking over where his wife sulkily sat, hiked directly past everyone to the fireplace where, legs planted wide, he began soaking up heat.

Betty smiled at her husband. He explained about Olmstead's car, then said, 'Apparently Calderon scared them off before they could cripple all the cars. Ralph took Calderon's Jaguar. I think it'll all be over soon now.' He slid an arm round his wife's thin waist and smiled.

She said there was a first-class breakfast waiting in the kitchen, and turned to tell the others, Mary-Katherine arose from her chair and without looking in her husband's direction at all, started for the kitchen. Olmstead, watching her go, gave his heavy shoulders a slight hitch then struck out behind her.

Betty and Mackenzie McAuliffe exchanged a look. He shook his head gently, then they too, headed for the kitchen.

15

The Advent of Dawn

They all looked tired and Emilio Calderon looked worse than tired but he was the most cheerful one of them even though it was forced.

Betty tried to brighten their mood too, and although it helped, the sustained effort was difficult for them both without much co-operation from the Olmsteads or Mackenzie, so in the end they finished their meal in either total silence or desultory conversation.

Frank Olmstead's attitude hadn't changed very much since he and Ralph had exchanged hot words some time earlier. When he spoke it was usually with sarcasm or irony.

And Dubois was not getting any better, which was obvious when they all went back into the living-room, replete if not rested. While Betty and Emilio worried over the butler, Mackenzie went out back for several more logs which he heaved into the large fireplace. After a bit their increased heat and light brightened the room somewhat, but as time dragged on everyone began to speculate about Ralph's success in reaching Brentsboro. Mackenzie reiterated an earlier statement of his to the effect that there had to be something seriously wrong with the connecting roadway.

Olmstead went over and spent some time puzzling over those two letters taken from the dead assassin. He was still doing this when, again without any warning, the lights came on. He blinked at the brightness and turned to suspiciously regard the nearest lamp. The others also peered at the sources of all that light as though either afraid it was a delusion, or afraid it wouldn't last.

But it did, and gradually they all accepted it. Mackenzie, associating one with the other, went into the study — which they had all been avoiding lately — and tried the telephone. It still was out of order so he returned, had a smoke by the blazing fire and watched his wife work over Dubois. Once, when she raised a strained, pale face, he smiled reassurance. She was anxious for the butler. Mackenzie's smile silently reiterated what he'd mentioned earlier: The man would survive, but at least for the time being there was nothing that could be done for him.

A sickly bluish dawn appeared and Frank Olmstead, smoking one of his cigars over by the front windows, said, 'Daylight in New England,' bitterness dripping from each word. 'Why in hell anyone would want to live in this part of the world is totally beyond my understanding. Look at that sky; here it is nearly summertime, and outside there it looks like Judgement Day.'

'It very well may be exactly that,' said his wife, throwing a barb in his direction, bringing Olmstead around slowly so that he could smoke and stand motionless, and stare at her.

There was a faint hum somewhere; an odd sound that seemed to come from the house itself. As it grew louder Olmstead, as baffled as the others, said, 'Fine, now it's going to turn out there's a time-bomb or something in the cellar.'

But it wasn't that kind of a sound at all and it steadily increased. While the wind had been howling they'd never have been able to detect it, but if the strange sound did little else for the time being, it at least made everyone aware that the wind was gone. Not entirely; there was still swaying shrubbery discernible out along the front of the house, but at least the wind was so diminished, or else had climbed so high overhead, it scarcely represented a hostile raw force any longer, and that was another indication that the wild and deadly night was over.

Mackenzie uttered an oath and hastened to the front door, threw it open and stepped out past the recessed part and began looking skyward. His wife at once left Dubois to Calderon's care and ran after him.

Mackenzie called to Olmstead. 'Come take a look at this.'

It was a two-seater helicopter and it was coming in low from the south-east.

It had the dingy sky just below its rotors and the wind up there, fiercer than it was at ground level, was pushing the vehicle in a sickening sway from side to side. But its pilot fought his controls so that even constantly off-course, he kept beating towards Masters Manor.

'Surely,' said Olmstead, 'the Brentsboro police department doesn't own one of *those* things.'

Mackenzie said, 'State police, not local police. Of course Brentsboro couldn't own one, they're too expensive.'

The helicopter, swaying with a gentle but unpleasant gait, kept on its course and at the same time it began dropping somewhat, as though to escape most of the fury of the wind, or perhaps because its pilot had Masters Manor well in sight and wished to seek out a landing site.

The helicopter finally got low enough to get clear of the wind's high fury and its swaying ceased. The pilot and his passenger were visible up there, but not recognisable. They dropped lower and beat on around the house from north to south at about roof-level, but when the people in the front door thought surely they'd land, the helicopter rose a bit and went darting over the rearward park like a great, noisy dragonfly.

Everyone went back inside and hastened to the glassed-in sunroom which offered a view of all the rearward country; at least as much of it as was visible in the grey new day.

The helicopter made passes from one side of the grounds to the other, obviously searching for something — or someone. It kept this up for some time, and meanwhile the daylight got a little better. Once, directly over the spot where something lumpy and black lay in the mud roughly midway between the manor house and the staff quarters, the helicopter hovered. Then it dropped to actual treetop level and went scooting out and back again.

Of course if anyone were down beneath the trees he'd be difficult to see unless he chose to be seen, which the man they were seeking most certainly would not choose.

Further, as Frank Olmstead grumbled

to the others in the sunroom, if the pilot had in mind catching that elusive assassin off-guard, he'd have to be deaf himself not to realise that vehicle of his made a frightful racket.

Then the helicopter jumped over the house and dropped down almost vertically to land out front where there was a broad, hard-surfaced driveway. Landing anywhere else after all the rain that had fallen the previous night might have been hazardous indeed.

Ralph Fielding unwound out of the plexi-glass bubble as those huge blades began their wind-down. Alighting from the opposite side of the helicopter was a beefy, helmeted individual wearing a fleece-lined coat and a pistol.

Olmstead, watching them come towards the house and evidently considering the beefy policeman, said, 'Well, now that the constabulary has arrived I must say he doesn't look very reassuring.'

Mary-Katherine said, 'What did you expect, the Royal Northwest Mounted Police complete with dog-teams?'

Olmstead ignored his wife.

Ralph Fielding grinned when he was close enough to make out the faces of the people in the gloomy doorway. They smiled back and stepped aside for the two men to come inside. It was still very raw and cold out, but the night-long fire inside had warmed up the entire large living-room, where Ralph introduced the pilot of that helicopter as a lieutenant of the State Police, Peter Collier.

Up close, Collier looked well-fed in a smooth, solid way. In contrast to the battered residents of Masters Manor he also looked very well rested, and fresh, Ralph had told him everything that had happened the night before, evidently, because as he nodded at each of the houseguests he let a long glance linger each time as though he were joining a face with some name in his mind. When the introductions were over he asked if anything had happened since Ralph had departed.

Nothing had, of course. Olmstead said again that the other assassin had been gone for some time now. He also deplored the breakdown of local communication equipment, professing the conviction that if they'd had access to the telephone they at least could have alerted the police to establish road-blocks.

Lieutenant Collier gazed with mild interest at Olmstead. 'Road-blocks?' he said.

Olmstead bobbed his head. 'Certainly. Don't tell me you haven't even heard of establishing road-blocks up here in God-forsaken New England?'

Lieutenant Collier kept looking from a blank face at Olmstead. 'We've heard of road-blocks, yes indeed. But what makes you think we'd need them here?'

Olmstead coloured. 'To prevent that damned murderer from completely escaping, that's why!'

'Mister Olmstead, that man isn't going to escape and we won't have to bother with road-blocks to ensure his capture.'

The others, even Calderon, looked at Lieutenant Collier. The policeman hadn't changed expression nor shown enthusiasm towards the chase, nor even any particular interest in the survivors of the night, either. He turned, pointed, and asked Ralph if that was the study. Ralph nodded and Lieutenant Collier walked off in that direction.

The moment he was gone Mackenzie said, 'Ralph . . . ?'

They all stood waiting for some kind of explanation Ralph gave it to them. 'The bridge is gone between here and the village. The police tried getting around it by going below the village, but that failed. They then tried reaching us on foot. They went out with the power-crew as far as that broken electrical line, but got turned back by mud slides. After that they called for a helicopter and it was brought over at great risk by a civilian pilot who then handed it over to Lieutenant Collier, and about that time I arrived in the village.'

Olmstead scowled perplexedly. 'The police couldn't get out *here*, but you could get down *there*?'

Ralph said, 'I left Emilio's car at the washout and rode a log *down* stream. That can be done. But if I'd been trying to come *up* stream to our side of the creek — now a great chocolate river, I never could have done it.'

Betty asked if they'd brought medical aid. They had; the policeman had it, but they'd also started a search for the local Brentsboro doctor and would have him on hand when Dubois and Calderon were flown out to the village.

Calderon looked at Ralph. 'No thank you,' he said. 'I saw the way he flew the helicopter coming in. I'll wait here until there is a better way to leave.'

Mackenzie smiled when the others did over Emilio's disinterest in succour, if it had to depend upon the lieutenant and his helicopter, but Mackenzie had a serious question to ask: 'Does he really believe that surviving assassin is still around?'

Ralph nodded. 'He believes it. So do I, after having a look around from the air. We couldn't locate the man, and although we know he has a car hidden somewhere around, we couldn't find that either. But I can tell you this much: he can't drive out of here, and he can't walk out either, without bumping into an alert they're putting on the air down at Brentsboro warning everyone with a radio to keep their doors and windows locked, and to admit no strangers to their houses, but to let the police know at once if someone strange appears.'

Mackenzie thought on that a bit, then said. 'Isn't there *some* way he can get out of here, Ralph? Perhaps the way you reached Brentsboro.'

Olmstead snorted. 'Sure, he can sprout wings and fly away.' He brushed Mackenzie's persistence aside and said, 'Fielding; what about the other one — the dead one?'

'He's still out there. Just before we landed Lieutenant Collier called back to State Police Headquarters in Brentsboro to give a description of the man, along with other things he saw from the air, and once Collier delivers the corpse, we'll have some definite answers.'

As though on cue, Peter Collier came out of the study, gently closed the door, as though Hugh Fielding were sleeping in there and shouldn't be disturbed, and without a word to the others walked right out of the house and down to the helicopter on the driveway. He climbed in, reached for his transmitting microphone and talked to Brentsboro as though he were the only person at Masters Manor.

Frank Olmstead said, 'Heinrich Himmler,' and stamped back to the fireplace although it was beginning to turn warm outside and that sooty sky was fading to a fish-belly shade of scaly grey. 'When will they fix that damned telephone?' he exclaimed. 'I'll hire my own chopper to get us out of here.'

'Not unless Heinrich Himmler says you can,' needled Mary-Katherine. 'Frank, he's coming back now from making his mysterious call. Why don't you tell him who you are and demand to know what he said out there?'

Olmstead did as he'd done on other occasions when his wife pinpricked him with her sarcasm. He looked at her in strong silence, then turned and ignored her entirely.

The others might have been accustomed to Mary-Katherine's moods except that their nerves were already rubbed raw.

But no one reproved her.

It was, as Mackenzie McAuliffe had repeatedly said, only a matter of hanging on a bit longer. With that kind of a promise held out to them, they could individually manage to endure, and so they did, ignoring Mary-Katherine when she was bitchy, and beginning to resent or dislike Lieutenant Collier whose brisk freshness was in contrast to their own weary disarray, and whose attitude of aloofness rubbed them very much the wrong way.

16

A New Day

Lieutenant Collier, whether anyone liked him or not, was efficient. He examined Dubois, pronounced Betty correct about a mild concussion, and gave the butler a pain-killing injection. Dubois sank into a profound sleep.

Emilio waved off Collier's attention saying he was coming along fine. He may have been but he didn't look it. He'd got by well enough in candle-light, and during that frightfully long night when everyone's mind was on other things, but in the brilliance of full light and when the others were able to look at Emilio objectively, he looked, as Mackenzie smilingly told him, 'Terrible.'

His face was swollen, the dark smudges beneath both eyes were getting darker, and when Collier insisted on removing

Betty's makeshift bandage to put on a fresh one, his gory wound was unpleasant to see.

He refused an injection from Lieutenant Collier, saying he felt well enough, all things considered, and preferred waiting until he could get professional assistance. He hadn't meant it as a slight and Lieutenant Collier, whose hide must have been very thick, did not take it that way. He simply put the large first-aid kit he'd brought back from the helicopter on a table, looked at them all, then said, 'I think I should take these two wounded men out, then come back for the rest of you. Unfortunately, I can only carry two at a time. Actually, the chopper is rated to only carry one passenger, plus the pilot, but I think we can make it safely with two. Mister Dubois and Mister — .'

'No,' interrupted Calderon. 'No thank you, Lieutenant.'

Collier turned stern. 'You need medical attention.' Calderon smiled apologetically. 'I prefer leaving some other way.'

'What other way, Mister Calderon? The

road is washed out, the creek between here and Brentsboro is a raging river and may not go down for a day or two. There is no other way.'

Emilio showed a stubborn streak by saying, 'I will stay here, Lieutenant,' and stopped smiling for as long as it took for Collier to understand he meant exactly what he said. Collier shrugged, putting a hint of scorn into it.

'The chopper is safe, Well, in that case I'll take Dubois out, then return with the doctor.'

Olmstead said, 'Meanwhile, what of that damned maniac out there, somewhere?'

Collier wasn't very concerned. 'My guess is that he's got his hands full, just trying to get away. But you folks should continue to stay inside and keep a sharp lookout.'

Frank Olmstead looked at Collier with barefaced exasperation, but he said no more until the policeman asked Ralph and Mackenzie to help him carry Dubois out to the helicopter. Then, watching the little group leave the house by the front doorway, Olmstead said, 'This is something straight out of a comic opera. The thick-headed policeman more concerned over a doped and supine wounded person, than he is over six potential murder victims. It's unbelievable.'

The helicopter ran up its motor stirring up a wind almost as fierce as the one the fugitives of Masters Manor had lived with the night before, then it sprang into the air and went clumsily beating its way back towards the broken, scaly sky in the general direction of Brentsboro.

Lieutenant Collier had invoked no restrictions on the people in the house for the best of all reasons; even if they were familiar with the countryside, they still were marooned. He may even have hoped some of them would try to flee, but none did.

However, Mackenzie wanted another look at the slain assassin, so, while Emilio and the two women remained behind, he and Frank Olmstead and Ralph Fielding went out through the steely daylight to the spot where the body lay.

They made a thorough search this time,

but came up with nothing other than a muddy handkerchief and a segment of road-map.

They found two bulletholes though, under the dead man's heavy sweater, and they also discovered that he was very well insulated by heavy clothing beneath his oilskins, indicating he — and presumably his companion who was still at large — had come prepared to spend that wild night without shelter.

The most unpleasant thing was moving the body towards the *porte-cochere* where they decently covered it with a piece of canvas, then stood looking all round.

Olmstead said, 'Fielding, where could the other one be?'

Ralph's answer showed he'd already considered this. 'Northward in the forest, westerly in the trees over there, or perhaps he got over to the neighbours. Otherwise, he's got to be watching us right this minute.'

Olmstead heard a noise and turned. A man and woman were picking their way across from the staff quarters towards the main house. Ralph passed them off easily; they were the housemaid, and her husband, who normally looked after the grounds. Those two stopped near the uprooted big tree and the man bitterly shook his head, then those two went on, disappearing around the back.

Mackenzie, standing thoughtfully silent, said suddenly, 'Is there a cellar beneath the staff quarters, Ralph?'

'Yes,' replied the new master of the Fielding estate. 'If you're wondering about the assassin being down there . . .' Ralph didn't finish it, he stood gazing over towards the distant residence with a narrowed, speculative glance.

Olmstead said, in dour protest, 'Listen, that's what taxpayers pay policemen for. Wait until Heinrich Himmler returns then let *him* go down there. In fact, let him search that whole blessed house. As far as I'm concerned its *his* job, not mine. Not yours either, either one of you.'

Mackenzie gazed briefly at Olmstead with a kind of quiet, disinterested expression, then seemed to cut the older man out of his thoughts entirely as he said, 'Ralph, suppose we go and have a look.'

Fielding hesitated, perhaps half believing as Olmstead believed, that the rewards, if any at all, couldn't possibly be commensurate with the risks. Whatever made him hesitate gave Betty McAuliffe a chance to come round where they were standing and say, 'Mrs. Olmstead and I have been listening to the radio. It helps, having the electricity on again. They are broadcasting a warning about an armed and dangerous man being somewhere within the vicinity of your place, Ralph. They interrupt the regular programmes every little while and issue their warning.' She looked at her husband, then said, 'The man can't possibly get clear if he hasn't already. The police will get him.'

Betty's innuendo, possibly based on a wife's knowledge of her man, was an indirect entreaty for Mackenzie to leave whatever happened now to the police. He smiled, understanding, and when Olmstead called the suggestion to go manhunting 'hare-brained and reckless' Mackenzie did not dispute it although the idea had been his in the first place.

Betty saw the lumpy thing nearby covered with canvas. She did not mention it and neither did any of the men. A little wind came along and ruffled their hair and made Betty hug herself for she was without a coat or jacket. Mackenzie put an arm round her and started back towards the house. As they walked, they spoke softly, indistinguishably, heads close. Olmstead looked pained but he said nothing. Ralph, walking with Olmstead, looked at the front of the house where wet stone, porous and aged, seemed to have met everything the storm had hurled at it with stolid, blind indifference. There was damage among the shrubbery along the house-front, and elsewhere as well, but the house itself seemed unharmed. Of course no one had as yet gone round to make a close inspection of that north wall where the big tree had struck and bounced off. It was improbable, considering the crushing blow that had befallen the wall around there, that the building had escaped some damage.

Inside, Emilio and Mary-Katherine

were quietly talking and the daylight was sufficient now for them to have turned off the lights, which was ironic whether anyone felt aware of it at the moment or not. They'd needed lights desperately in the bleakest hours of the deadly night, and had been denied them. Then, when the electrical service had finally been restored, not to be interrupted again, they could turn it off.

Emilio disappeared into the kitchen and returned with a tray of glasses full of tomato juice. It was a pleasant surprise. Even Frank Olmstead, in the act of lighting one of his cigars, looked less disgruntled than usual and thanked Calderon as he accepted his glass.

Later, when everyone was sitting relaxed, awaiting whatever ensued, Calderon beckoned Mackenzie McAuliffe over and quietly led him out into the sunroom, then around into Hugh Fielding's study by the side, connecting door, and there he showed Mackenzie something that perhaps Lieutenant Collier had discovered but which no one else had found the night before in the unpleasant darkness.

The telephone wire running from Hugh Fielding's desk along an ornamental base-shoe and terminating where a small metal box was screwed to the wood, lay limply parted two inches from the connecting juncture inside the small metal box screwed to the base-board.

Mackenzie started.

Calderon was quiet until satisfied McAuliffe understood the implication, then he said, 'The first time, I believe, the wire was cut elsewhere. Perhaps somewhere a long distance from the house. But when that break was discovered and fixed, someone then broke it here, *inside* the house.'

Mackenzie looked closely, then knelt and picked up the broken wire. It had been torn, not cut; at least it looked badly mauled and bruised. He straightened up and said, 'Emilio, that second time . . . 'He shook his head. 'I don't see how it could have been done that second time. As I recall we were all in the room. Ralph was talking to the telephone-man at the other end.' He looked with puckered concentration, at Calderon.

Emilio said, 'It seems a lifetime ago, doesn't it? I also tried to recall where everyone was standing when the telephone went dead in Ralph's hand.' Calderon humped his shoulders, then dropped them, indicating he had had the same difficulty Mackenzie was now having. Then he said, 'I came to a conclusion.'

McAuliffe said, 'Yes?'

'This broken wire only confirms that someone *inside* the house has been involved right from the beginning.'

Mackenzie thoughtfully bent to examine the broken wire again, then he said, 'Get a screwdriver. Ralph will know where one is. We can repair this thing, unless there is another break we don't know about.'

Calderon left the room and moments later, evidently informed, Olmstead and Ralph Fielding appeared in the doorway. The women did not accompany them. After all, Hugh Fielding's corpse was still beneath the lumpy blanket on the sofa.

Olmstead saw the break, as did Ralph, and each of them reacted as Mackenzie had done; they tried to guess who had been standing over near the wall when the telephone had gone dead in Ralph's hand. They even argued a little. Olmstead saying he thought Calderon had been standing over there and Ralph saying he'd thought it had been Olmstead.

The older man's voice arose indignantly. 'Like hell; I was over near the door. I remember that perfectly. I was trying to figure out what the man at the other end was saying from your remarks. I was smoking a cigar.'

Calderon returned with two screw-drivers. After that the guesswork about who had been standing where, by bringing down a heel, they could have broken the connection, ended. The four men were interested in seeing whether Mackenzie would make an adequate repair or not.

He made it, but only by securing additional slack in the wire, by loosening it along the base-shoe. The actual connection itself was elemental; a crooked eyelet that encircled a small copper screw.

When Mackenzie finished he pointed.

'Try the phone,' he said.

Ralph picked it up, listened, nodded at Mackenzie and said, standing holding the thing away from his head, 'Perfect dial-tone.'

Olmstead held out a hand. 'Let me make a call. I'll call my office in New York and have a charter-copter sent up here to get us out of this place.'

Ralph did not relinquish the telephone. Instead, he slowly dialled the number of the police station down in Brentsboro to ascertain whether Lieutenant Collier was on his way back yet or not. He was, said a man's voice, and the Road Department was also heading up to see about some kind of temporary span for bringing everyone out over the county roads.

Ralph broke the connection, handed the telephone to Olmstead and turned to consider Calderon and McAuliffe. 'Won't be long now,' he told them.

17

A Mysterious Stranger

What was a long period of time or a short period of time was, like so many things, relative. For example, the entire night from the moment they had all retired until the moment Lieutenant Collier had arrived in his unorthodox helicopter, had been about nine or ten hours, but by the subsequent statements of the survivors of that night, the entire thing had lasted a long lifetime.

For one of them at least, it had been the termination of a lifetime, and that was what Lieutenant Collier was most interested in when he got back, bringing a youngish-pleasant medical practitioner who offered tranquillisers to Betty and Mary-Katherine — both of whom declined them — then took Emilio Calderon to the kitchen where a horrified housemaid fled to make the beds upstairs as soon as she saw Emilio's wound.

Ralph, who had been closest when his father had been shot to death, had to tell his story twice so that Lieutenant Collier might check each detail of it. Collier proved to be an endlessly patient man. He interrogated them in a group then separately in the study, he picked up little things and dwelt upon them, analysing, dissecting, trying to weave some kind of pattern.

It was, Ralph said, the motive that had him utterly baffled. Collier admitted that if they knew the motive, of course it would probably help immeasurably, but since they didn't seem to know it, they could only assume that it was a very serious matter to *someone*; people did not spend a night out in one of the wildest storms of the early springtime season, and deliberately shoot a man to death, then bottle up a half dozen other people all night long, without what was, at least to the culprits, a very good motive.

Olmstead said tartly that instead of

standing around in the living-room of Masters Manor, if Collier went out and pushed an aggressive search of the estate, particularly the staff quarters, he might find someone who could explain everything.

Lieutenant Collier sourly contemplated Frank Olmstead. It would perhaps be some little time before Collier discovered what Olmstead's night-long companions already knew: He was just naturally antagonistic towards anyone who sought to unravel their common nightmare.

When Emilio returned, more jaunty in a professional bandage, followed by the youthful doctor, Lieutenant Collier swooped; he took Calderon into the study and spent a half an hour interrogating Emilio, longer, except in the case of Ralph Fielding, than he'd detained any of the others.

When Calderon returned he and Mackenzie exchanged a look. McAuliffe was curious as to whether or not Calderon had told Collier about the broken telephone wire.

He had told him. When they found

themselves slightly apart from everyone else, Mackenzie asked and Calderon answered. But he added something that made McAuliffe gaze upon him with quick interest.

'Yes, I explained how I saw the broken wires this morning. He also wanted to know who had repaired them — who would have that kind of knowledge. Then he told me we were all in the study at that time, except for Mary-Katherine.' Calderon pulled a quirk of a crooked smile. 'You see, the man is extremely thorough.'

Mackenzie thought a moment then said, 'By George, that's right. I remember now. Mary-Katherine was sulking because Olmstead wouldn't let her go hoist one at the bar. She was sitting in that big chair facing the fireplace.'

Calderon shrugged. He did not, he said, remember as clearly where everyone had been, but it had never crossed his mind Mary-Katherine could, or would, have been the person to break the telephone wire.

Mackenzie eyed the Central American

from an expressionless face. Obviously, he did not share Calderon's romantic opinion of Mary-Katherine.

Ralph came over where they were standing to say he had telephoned his father's business associates down in New York to verify Olmstead's tale, and it had checked out perfectly.

'The man was telling the truth,' said Ralph, sounding disappointed, 'my father and he were preparing to form a new company.'

'Could that have any connotations?' asked Mackenzie, and Ralph shook his head.

'The agency people in New York were shocked at my father's death. It was a little early in the day to drop that on them. They've promised to re-evaluate everything in the files and let me know later on if they turn up anything.'

Collier went outdoors but no one missed him for a bit because he'd used the kitchen and rear porch instead of the front door, to leave the house. Mary-Katherine said she thought he was going looking for the unknown assassin. Her husband snorted.

'It's damned near eight o'clock and daylight. That killer is long gone.'

'He couldn't be,' said Betty McAuliffe. 'Lieutenant Collier said the man's bottled up within something like a three mile radius.'

The only sympathetic comment came from Emilio, who said he thought Collier would have been wiser to enlist the help of the men in the house, because *if* that assassin actually was out there, Lieutenant Collier might end up like Hugh Fielding.

But Collier surprised them all by returning shortly to elicit help at carrying Hugh Fielding out to the helicopter where the corpse was strapped hard and fast to one of the landing skids. Already strapped upon the opposite skid was the canvas-shrouded body of the dead assassin. Collier had evidently been busy.

He climbed into the helicopter, waved, ran up the motor and took off forcing Ralph, Olmstead and Mackenzie McAuliffe to turn and hunch their bodies against the violent slip-stream from the whirling rotor-blades. Olmstead was loudly condemnatory, when he was at last able to speak.

'What in the hell,' he exclaimed, shaking a big fist at the airborne helicopter, 'is so important that he has to take those corpses out ahead of the living? I tell you that man is the most obnoxious, the most arrogant, the most irritating human being I've seen in ages.' He glared. 'Fielding, of all the policemen, why did you have to pick that one!'

They went back as far as the *porte-cochere* where Mackenzie offered Ralph his cigarette packet, then the pair of them lit up off the same match. Olmstead's antagonism remained strong. He said that as soon as the charter helicopter arrived that he'd instructed his people down in New York to arrange for, he was damned well going to leave Masters Manor with his wife regardless of what anyone said or did, and that included Lieutenant Collier.

Ralph turned to gaze out between the staff quarters and main house. That uprooted large tree lay partially visible, its soil bound great mushroom of a root system nearly as tall as a man. He suddenly caught his breath, then expelled it very softly and spoke.

'Turn very slowly, you two, and look at the fringe of trees to the right, or northward, close to the front of the staff quarters.'

Olmstead and McAuliffe obeyed. The older man said, 'What, I don't see anything,' then he too suddenly caught his breath with a little rasp of audible sound. Mackenzie didn't speak, didn't move, didn't indicate by look or sound that he'd seen anything, until, with all three of them silent in the gloomy shadows under the *porte-cochere*, he finally spoke in a very low and quiet voice to ask whether or not Ralph still had that long-barrelled pistol in his waistband.

Ralph did have. Lieutenant Collier had made some slighting remark about them all carying guns, and their reaction had been to stonily return his look and continue to carry their guns.

'Can you hit him from here with it?' asked Mackenzie, still in a tone so soft it had no depth nor echo.

Ralph thought he could although he confessed that for a pistol, his or any other, the range was really excessive. In his case that long barrel might help.

'No,' said Frank Olmstead. 'How do you know it's not some neighbour coming over to see how much damage was done over here? You can't just up and take a pot-shot when you can't even see his face. I won't allow it.'

The object of this lethal conversation was visible, primarily because whether he knew it or not, there was a large very pale bush at his back, and he was consequently limned perfectly in the pale saffron morning light.

As Olmstead had said, the man was too distant to be seen distinctly, but on the other hand, he was watching the main house with what even at that distance was wholehearted concentration, one hand lying lightly upon a tree, the rest of his body bent slightly from the waist in the manner of a person straining to see or hear.

Ralph had a suggestion to offer. 'All we'd have to do is step to the right and we'd be cut off from his sight by the staff quarters. Then go around the front of it and up the north side, and be no more than perhaps two or three hundred feet from the man.'

Olmstead snorted. 'And what good would that do? That's all open ground from the back of the staff quarters to those trees where he's standing. How do we rush him without being seen at once — then he'll disappear in that lousy forest.'

'That's what he'd do if we were *lucky*,' muttered Mackenzie, leaning his head upon one hand and squinting in the direction of that distant, mysterious figure. 'If we were *not* lucky, he could stand up there across the clearing and enjoy a little target shooting at our expense.'

Ralph was exasperated. 'So what do we do — stand here and let him escape?'

'He can't,' growled Olmstead. 'You

heard what Collier said.'

Ralph's retort was swift and angry. 'To hell with what Collier said. *I* know the countryside a damned sight better than he does.'

The other two looked around. Ralph inclined his head. 'It was asinine for Collier to say that killer over there couldn't escape. All he had to do was head due west or due south.'

'He'd be afoot,' growled Olmstead.

'Not for long,' retorted Ralph. 'There are farms and other estates in both directions. He could get a car at any of them.' Ralph eased forward to pick out that distant, motionless figure again, then with a grunt of satisfaction he eased around behind Olmstead, behind McAuliffe, sidling to the right until he was hidden from that distant watcher. McAuliffe thought a moment, then sidled away to leave Olmstead alone in the murky gloom of the *porte-cochere*.

It was somewhat as it had been in the howling darkness hours earlier for McAuliffe and Ralph Fielding, except that now there was more light, and also, they definitely *knew*, had *seen*, their enemy.

They reached the front of the staff quarters without effort but when they paused over there Frank Olmstead came loping up. He had made no attempt to join any of the other expeditions up to now so the younger men gazed at him, each with his private thoughts, and Olmstead, conceivably surmising some of that speculation said, 'This is just as crazy as going out last night to save the butler. But at least I can *see* this morning, and that ensures me an even break.'

Ralph led over to the edge of the staff quarters, which was considerably higher in front than in back due to a slope in the land, but something occurred that blew the entire undertaking.

The helicopter came beating its way back swinging in low and sounding — even somewhat resembling — an erratic egg-beater.

Ralph thrust his head around the side of the building, let out a great, heartfelt curse and stepped fully out facing northward. The motionless watcher up there was gone, evidently frightened off by the return of the helicopter.

Olmstead shook his fist at the aircraft but the younger men simply stood gazing over where their prey had been. McAuliffe asked what the chances would be of finding that man again if they rushed across the empty rearward park and got into the trees about where the stranger had disappeared.

Ralph outlined the obstacles, which were mainly those of any tangled thicket with trees all around. Meanwhile, the helicopter landed out front and Frank Olmstead went angrily striding off in that direction.

Mackenzie, looking at Ralph, suddenly smiled. 'You know; I actually think Olmstead would have done it this time.'

Ralph nodded. 'I think so. But I'll tell you something else I think: That stranger was watching the house for some particular person to come out, or for a particular signal.'

McAuliffe's smile winked out. He

studied the yonder woods for a bit, then turned back as the growing voice of Frank Olmstead was audible over where he was striding with Lieutenant Collier towards the staff quarters.

18

The Manhunt Shapes Up

Collier had a biting observation to make in refutation to Ralph Fielding's defensive remark that he knew the countryside well enough to also know that killer could escape. Collier said sourly, 'I didn't mean, Mister Fielding, that this killer, or whatever he is, was entirely limited in the scope of his movements by the washed out road. I meant that other law enforcement officers have been brought in from the south and west, by car, and have been deployed to sweep the countryside in this direction as they approach.'

Ralph, Mackenzie, even Frank Olmstead, were surprised, perhaps slightly chagrined for having thought Collier a far less competent policeman than he was turning out to be.

He also said, looking almost scornfully at the three men in front of the staff quarters, that if they *had* tried to track, or in some other manner pursue that stranger, there was a very excellent opportunity that they'd encounter some of the oncoming screen of possemen, and get shot for their pains. Then Collier turned, glanced over where the stranger had been, turned in a different direction and considered the back of the main house.

'What would he have been watching?' he mused.

Ralph offered his earlier suggestion. 'He was waiting for someone, I think, or possibly he was waiting for another flashlight-signal.'

Collier looked at Ralph with a slow nod. 'Possibly. But if you three were out here, then that would mean either the Mexican or the two women would have to signal, wouldn't it?'

'He's not a Mexican,' spoke up Ralph. 'I'm not sure he'd like being called one either. As for the other — you may be wrong, Lieutenant. That stranger did not know Olmstead, McAuliffe and I were out here. It may even be the very fact that we *were* out here, that would account for the fact that no one seemed to signal him. He certainly stood over there a long time before fading out.'

Collier offered a thin smile. 'Gallant of you, Mister Fielding, including yourself among the suspects.'

Ralph coloured slightly but had no more to say. He stepped clear and started back towards the front of the house.

For a moment Olmstead and McAuliffe stood gazing at Collier, then Olmstead said, 'Lieutenant, it may come as a surprise to you, but this attitude you've shown since first arriving here is going a very long way towards alienating everyone.'

Collier was unruffled. 'I have a job to do, Mister Olmstead, and I do it the best way I know how.'

'In that case,' retorted the older man, 'unles you show more intelligence in our trouble than you've shown so far in knowing how to handle people, there's not a chance of you doing anything here but wasting everyone's time.' Olmstead stepped past and started towards the house in the wake of Ralph.

Lieutenant Collier started to speak, to hurl some comment after Olmstead. Mackenzie McAuliffe interrupted him.

'Olmstead is exactly right, Lieutenant Collier. If you have some ridiculous idea that being a policeman has given you some kind of preference over the rest of humanity, forget it. There are, actually, fewer rungs any lower on the acceptable social ladder than the one occupied by policemen.'

Collier turned and regarded McAuliffe. Collier had now been given two very candid views within a space of moments by men who were a few notches above the ordinary. A wise man, even a policeman, might have been guided by the preponderance opinion. Whatever Peter Collier thought was evidenced by nothing he said or did, but when McAuliffe stood there without moving giving Collier stare for stare, the initiative was Collier's. He turned and started back towards the main house without another word.

There was a telephone call for Collier when he reached the house. Olmstead, already in the living-room and angrily demanding of the four walls where that chartered helicopter was that he'd called for, declined the smoke someone offered him and said waiting around Masters Manor in daylight was turning out to be even harder than waiting around in it the night before when it seemed probable they would all be assassinated.

Ralph and Mackenzie heard Collier speaking curtly to someone on the telephone in the study. Collier told whoever it was on the telephone with him that he wanted the information swiftly; that it might be the difference between arresting a murderer and letting one get away.

Ralph looked at Mackenzie with a trite little smile. 'Sounded very dramatic,' he said, 'and since I can't find that much imagination in our private Hawkshaw, I'd say the man's got hold of something.'

When Collier returned from the study he left the house without a word to any of the people in it and was gone for some little while. Olmstead's slow simmer came to a boil. He called his

New York office and was loudly abusive. He was informed, he said after making that telephone call, that the helicopter he'd chartered had been ordered to land at Brentsboro by the police. The pilot, in reporting back to his own people, informed them the police had told him he would be able to fly on in to Masters Manor shortly, but that right at the moment there was a concerted manhunt going on and they'd prefer not having the helicopter disrupt things, which it most certainly would do by driving the fugitive to ground just by an overflight.

'Ridiculous,' stormed Olmstead. 'Absolutely preposterous. Collier told us there was a skirmish-line or something like that sweeping towards Masters Manor.'

'A dragnet?' suggested Emilio, evidently liking that phrase because he smiled over it.

'Call it what you will,' snapped Frank Olmstead. 'In any case, helicopter or no helicopter, they're bound to flush that killer if they've got the place surrounded, and of course providing he wasn't gone before they set it up. What possible harm can one helicopter flying over cause?'

No one answered him. No one felt particularly impelled to do so. Slightly apart from the others, Mackenzie and Ralph looked wryly at Olmstead. Ralph said, 'I think it's going to be a minor miracle if I don't shut him up one of these times with a fist in his mouth — *my* fist.'

Mackenzie offered that tired smile again. 'What would you gain, excepting torn knuckles? Collier may leave a lot to be desired — most policemen do — but if they have enough peoplc out there to saturate the area, they will succeed.'

Mackenzie was right but until Lieutenant Collier returned to the house to rush to the study and make another of his mysterious telephone calls no one seemed to believe it.

When he emerged this time, instead of returning out of doors he stood a moment with a little metal receiver in one hand and surveyed the quiet people watching him from various positions around the living-room. Then he said, his tone slightly less arrogant than it had been up until now, 'There is a pretty good chance that we've got him pinned down.'

'Where?' Ralph demanded at once.

'Northwesterly, in those doggoned trees up there.'

Ralph nodded. He knew the area well. 'I think I'd better go with you,' he said, and when Collier's face assumed its old look of heavy scorn Ralph said, 'You won't find him unless I do.'

Collier's lips lifted sardonically. 'Oh? And why not, Mister Fielding?'

'Because there are four caves over there and if he finds one, or perhaps already knew where one was, you and your people could walk right over the top of him.' Ralph smiled the same way he often did when feeling hostile, showing his dislike, then turned, sauntered to a chair and sat down. 'On second thoughts you'll probably find him, Lieutenant. After all, you *do* have a great posse, you said, and you don't like civilian interference.'

Ralph lit a cigarette, deliberately turned his back on Collier and began speaking to Betty McAuliffe who was sitting on the same sofa two injured men had used the night before.

Collier's neck reddened. His little humourless eyes narrowed. The hand holding the receiver whitened from squeezing. He was angry and seemed to be groping for some appropriate retort.

McAuliffe said, 'Come along, Ralph,' and went across to stand by the front door.

Collier said nothing. Neither did any of the others. McAuliffe's move had been obviously designed to bring young Fielding back into the matter without having anything to do with the policeman. Ralph turned, met McAuliffe's patient look, then finally rose and crossed to Mackenzie's side. The pair of them left the house without a glance at Collier, who at once started after them but Frank Olmstead halted him at the door with a short, hard comment.

'If you think you're so secure in your job, Lieutenant, that inefficiency can't prove otherwise, just keep on acting like you've been acting around here.'

Collier slammed the door as he went

outside where McAuliffe and Fielding were pausing a moment to make certain their weapons were still operative. There, coming up to them, Lieutenant Collier said, 'Mister Fielding, where exactly are those caves?'

Ralph looked pityingly at the policeman. Have you seen that stretch of forest, Lieutenant?'

'Yes.'

'Then you must realise there are no road signs among the trees. How the hell do you expect me to explain where the caves are?'

'Are they man-made, Mister Fielding?'

'That I can't answer. They are very old and are in the rocks. If men made them, I've always supposed they had to be prehistoric men, but even on that score no one has ever seemed very clear. As a boy I used to play in them, although my father didn't like the idea.'

'Are they visible to people walking through the forest?'

'Two are. The other two have underbrush growing in front of them. I'd hazard a guess that if the fugitive stumbled onto one of them it would have to be one of the visible ones.' Ralph pushed the target-pistol back into his waistband and looked at McAuliffe. 'No need for you to come along, Mackenzie; you're tired and if there's really a posse out there you won't be needed. Why don't you stay at the house and get some rest?'

Mackenzie said, 'We're both tired,' and grinned ruefully.

Ralph nodded and struck out, leading the way. They had to pass the staff quarters, cross the soggy fields northward, turn westerly after they reached firmer ground, and all around them the grey daylight was both raw and inhospitable.

The sky was beginning to brighten with a healthier glow, however, off in the distant east. It was fair to assume that before this day was spent the sun would shine, but right at the moment the three men trudged across spongy earth and damp grass, the day was leaden, to match their moods.

Lieutenant Collier spoke little. Once, shortly before they reached the fringe of trees, he called someone on his receiver. Ralph and Mackenzie heard him give their approximate location along with a warning that that they would shortly be in the forest and the possemen were to be so informed.

Later, just as they passed through the first line of trees, the little receiver made its buzzing sound to indicate someone wanted to speak to Collier. He told Ralph and Mackenzie to stop, then he spoke his name into the little intercom and stood in a posture of absorbed interest for a long moment. Afterwards, when he'd broken the connection he said, 'Well; there is a ballistics report on the bullet that killed your father, Mister Fielding. Not that it will be of much use unless we find the gun — and the man who was holding it when the shot was fired. But there is something else . . . That man you people shot it out with has been identified as one Franklin Delano Bordhese.'

Ralph's expression, like Mackenzie's, must have registered the sudden surprise both men felt. Collier gazed at them then nodded.

'The same last name as in the old newspaper clipping. That's interesting isn't it?'

Mackenzie said, 'It's not a very common name, Lieutenant.'

Collier smiled. 'True. And it's part of the puzzle; but without other parts it isn't going to help us much. Suppose we continue our search for those caves, Mister Fielding, and possibly we'll turn up another part of the puzzle. That's all police work is, you know, feeling around until you have a piece of something in your hand, then feeling around until you locate another part of the puzzle. After a while you fit one piece into another piece, and from there some kind of pattern emerges.'

It was the longest speech Collier had made, and it was quite civil. Very probably the candid hostility of the people at Masters Manor had reached through his professional density and brought something of the man himself into the open.

Ralph turned and struck out into the forest. Almost at once what little steely light there had been, became diluted darkness with a clammy chill added to it, but at least there was no longer any wind, so each step they took had a soggy, abrasive sound that was audible because there were no other sounds to drown it out.

19

Pieces of a Puzzle

Twice Collier contacted someone by means of his receiver and twice he informed Ralph and Mackenzie there was no sign at all of the fugitive out where the possemen were closing in, through the forest. Collier was of the opinion the man had to be in one of the caves.

Ralph went to the nearest cave first, which happened to be one of those dark, clammy holes whose front was completely obscured by both underbrush and trees. It was clearly demonstrable without even entering the hole that no one had been inside since quite some time before the storm; the mouth of the opening was nearly waist high with undisturbed but mouldy and soggy debris.

The second cave was larger and exposed, but only providing a person approached from the east, for otherwise the opening was invisible in a low, rocky promontory of something like ten feet, over which a flourishing bush with inch-long, sharp thorns kept vigil.

It was difficult here to say whether anyone had been through the front opening or not because there was a smooth stone entry-way that ran out into the surrounding forest for a considerable distance. There were no bushes growing through that layer of thick stone, and if there had been muddy footsteps upon it, they had been washed away, evidently, for when Ralph stopped and pointed towards the black hole and beyond that, to the blacker depths of this cave, he said, 'Another blank I'm afraid.'

Collier was not a man to accept the evidence his eyes presented without substantiating it by a prowl about. Ralph shrugged, lit a cigarette and watched Collier enter the cave. Mackenzie asked what was inside. The answer was indifferently given.

'Nothing, really, but a branch-off about fifteen feet ahead, and two rooms, one to the left, one to the right. I used to lie in there as a youngster and waylay horribly painted and bespangled Red Indians who searched for me with tomahawks and great knives. Of course I put them all down with unerring aim from my absolutely trustworthy, imaginative rifle.'

Mackenzie smiled, looked round, found a moderately dry rock and sat upon it. He said, 'For some bizarre reason I no longer feel bushed.'

Ralph nodded; it was rather like getting one's second wind, actually, when from the secret wellspring deep down one got an additional infusion of energy.

Collier emerged rubbing his head. He'd neglected to duck down at one of the entrances. Warning him hadn't occurred to Ralph. As a lad he hadn't been tall enough to be in peril, and since manhood he hadn't entered the old cave.

'Nothing,' said Collier, still massaging the bump. 'Let's get along.'

Collier's receiver began making its rattlesnake sound. He threw up a hand to halt Mackenzie and Ralph and spoke shortly to someone, then pocketed the receiver and pointed almost due westerly. 'They've found tracks off there a mile or so, I'd judge, from where we are.'

Ralph said, 'Interesting. That's where one of the caves is. Are they following the tracks?'

'Yes. They'll be driving him directly towards us — unless of course that cave intervenes.'

Ralph smiled enigmatically, did not confirm nor deny the location of the cave, and turned to go plunging off in a westerly direction.

Once, crossing a muddy little clearing, they encountered sunlight. None of them had felt the increased warmth although it had been building up all around them for some little while now. It was difficult to feel especially warm when one was walking on feet that were saturated with cold mud.

Suddenly, they could see open ground on their right and Mackenzie asked about it. Ralph said it was the arable land of their neighbour, a successful farmer. He also said there was an old post-and-rider fence off through the trees there which they wouldn't be able to see until they got right up to it, because the fence was very old and almost completely covered by wild rose vines.

This seemed to turn Collier's interest in a different direction. He asked how far the farmhouse was, and upon learning it was roughly a mile, or perhaps slightly less, he said that when they met up with the others he'd send someone over there, providing they didn't run their man to earth beforehand.

Mackenzie was puzzled by the fact, that if indeed the fugitive were still around, he had demonstrated what Mackenzie called, 'errant stupidity.' Collier was sour about that.

'If criminals were intelligent, Mister McAuliffe, they'd hardly be criminals, would they?'

It was one of those annoyingly snide remarks Collier was in the habit of making, and while enough people believed it to lend the cliche a sound of ringing truth, anyone with an ounce of scepticism might suspect that it wasn't true at all.

Mackenzie ignored the policeman and

said, 'Ralph, you said he could escape southerly or westerly, so I'm baffled.'

Ralph was agreeable. 'I am too. Except for one thing; he seemed to want to talk to someone back there at the house, or else he was waiting for them to join him, when he stood out there this morning. Perhaps he waited too long, not suspecting the police were moving in all around him.'

Collier said, 'That's the idea, Mister Fielding. I hope it works.'

They passed through a particularly bad stretch of forest. Ordinarily such thriving undergrowth didn't really overrun the area until full summer was upon the countryside, and in fact although there were leafy new shoots, most of the thorny tangle they were forced to traverse was left over from years past.

It made, as Ralph pointed out, an ideal covert for wildlife, which his father cherished, and which their neighbour, the farmer, also felt was entitled to a private sanctuary.

As though to support Ralph's comments, and doubtless alarmed by their noisy progress a great blue doe sprang from the heart of a man-high thicket, cleared the highest branches with ease, and was gone in a flash, until all the startled men saw of her was the quick flicker of her two-toned flag — her tail.

Under the circumstances, suspecting an armed killer was close, it was pardonable that the three men reacted identically by dropping forward into a crouch and reaching for their weapons.

Collier recovered first, swore, then motioned for Ralph to push onward.

They found the third cave, eventually, and had only just approached its large, black opening, when a man's quiet voice said, 'Steady right where you are, boys. Don't turn around.'

Mackenzie sighed, otherwise the three of them stood like stone. Finally, the calm voice said, 'You there — taller feller with the tweed jacket — turn round so's I can see your face.'

Ralph was the only one wearing a tweed coat. He turned. There was nothing to see but dense undergrowth. The quiet voice spoke again.

'Sorry. That's you isn't it, Mister Fielding?'

Ralph nodded. Collier turned very slowly, looking indignant. The invisible man rose suddenly from the heart of a spider-like bush and leaned upon a shotgun.

'Ames,' he said, smiling at Ralph. 'Deputy Ames from Port Royal, Mister Fielding. 'Thought I recognised you.' The deputy sheriff gazed upon Lieutenant Collier with dignified calm. 'Had to be a little careful,' he explained. There was three of you.' He stepped out of his hiding place and strolled on over. Deputy Ames was a tall, rawboned, weathered New Englander with the lean lips, the level eyes, and the unruffled demeanour that went with his type of man.

Collier was a trifle short, annoyed no doubt at being caught flatfooted like that. He said, 'I suppose you're part of the posse, Deputy Ames.' The New Englander evidently did not know Collier; he studied him now with candid interest and nodded without speaking.

Collier then asked where the other

men were and Ames pointed in three directions and said, 'There was some sign of people being in the forest back there. They'll be coming a little slower than I did.' Ames smiled lazily. 'I used to poach in these woods, Lieutenant; I figured I'd just come on up here and lay in wait.'

Collier was cryptic. 'If you'll go and bring in the others, Deputy, we three will wait here for them.'

Ames nodded in that same laconic manner again, shot Ralph a slightly amused look, turned and went back into the forest without a sound.

Mackenzie grinned. 'Yankee New Englander,' he mused. 'They are a breed apart, eh?'

Collier did not answer and Mackenzie had not expected him to since he was grinning in Ralph's direction. For a moment Ralph watched the Lieutenant approach the cave opening before he said, 'A breed apart is right, Mackenzie.' Then, louder, he said, 'Lieutenant — mind your head.'

Collier gave him a sour look and entered the cave.

Somewhere, a goodly distance off, a dog barked. Ralph turned to listen. Seeing Mackenzie's expression of enquiry he said, 'Over at the farmhouse, I think. Probably some of the possemen.'

The barking grew fainter, as though the dog were retreating, and after a bit it stopped altogether. The sun began burning through the treetops sprinkling a kind of cathedral brightness all around. There would be steam rising from the sodden land when the heat got high enough but for the time being Ralph and Mackenzie lounged in increasing warmth finding it both relaxing and pleasant.

'Bordhese,' mused Ralph aloud, as though repeating the name only for his own benefit. 'What would the connection be?'

'The newspaper article hinted at some kind of contraband,' said Mackenzie. 'But the byline was from Italy, transmitted to the U.S. by wire service. What would a little coastal tramp ship in Italy have to do with the New England back-country, I wonder? What would this other Bordhese be carrying that clipping in his wallet for?'

Ralph was reasonably sure of one thing. 'There is a connection. Like Collier said — we need more parts of the puzzle to make any sense from this, Mackenzie.'

As though summoned by the mention of his name, the Lieutenant of police came out of the cave with something in his hand. It was an old, ragged blanket. He flung it down and struck his palms together as though to cleanse them.

Ralph went closer and looked at the old blanket. It might have belonged to the fugitive but he said it probably had been in the cave for a good many years, judging from its rotting condition. He also said that from time to time boys used the caves as secret meeting places for their games, exactly as he'd done as a youth.

Collier poked the blanket with his toe. 'That's all there was in that hole. It didn't belong to the man we want in any case, because there are no signs of anyone having been in there for years. Dust and leaves and rats' nests are all over the place, undisturbed.'

That dog started barking again in the northerly distance. Collier became very interested. About that time three men armed with shotguns or rifles came noisily from the direction Deputy Ames had gone, but the deputy was not among them.

Lieutenant Collier knew two of the men, both State Policemen with the black stripe down their field-grey trousers which was regulation. He curtly introduced Fielding and McAuliffe, then asked if someone was out there in the direction the dog was barking.

One of the newcomers said, 'I gave Sergeant Northcutt my receiver, Lieutenant. He's out there with a couple of other troopers. He is to make a thorough search of the farmhouse then call us here.'

Collier had no fault to find with this strategy although he didn't look too pleased with it.

The barking dog stopped again, and the only sound was the crunching of feet as a line of men began closing in on the cave-area from farther back in the woods.

Now, the heat began building up noticeably. It seemed improbable that after that wild and uncontrolled storm of the night before, summer could ever make itself felt again, yet it was doing just exactly that. In fact, through the stiff limbs overhead a pale, clear sky was visible.

20

Capture!

The call came within a short space of time and Collier was informed that the men with Sergeant Northcutt had the fugitive cornered in a shed near the farm buildings.

At once McAuliffe's spirits revived considerably. Even Lieutenant Collier acted as if regenerated. He smiled as he asked Ralph to lead the way, and even when they all had to clamber over that weed-choked old rotting fence, which was a delicate and uncomfortable undertaking, there was no grumbling.

Beyond the fence there were additional woods for perhaps a quarter mile but beyond that was one huge, slightly rolling field. Here, even the sunniest of dispositions faltered because the ploughed earth sucked each foot down a good six inches and it required genuine effort to walk at all.

Ralph and Mackenzie were not wearing boots like the others, therefore, along with accumulating great gobbets of dark, heavy mud with each step which had to be kicked loose, their shoes quickly filled with the stuff, which also went up their trouser-legs, inside as well as outside.

The only rewarding aspect of this uncomfortable hike was that when they finally saw the buildings, they kept looking closer in the sunshine, and in fact they even saw a number of men, small as yet in the distance, but men none the less, standing around near the large red-brick farmhouse. It appeared that there were at least a dozen men over there; sunshine flashed off armament.

Ralph said he thought the farmer and his three sons were among those men. He told Collier the farmer, whose name was Brewster, was not only a very successful and moderately wealthy man, but also had a reputation for being tough and resourceful when antagonised. Collier's reply was a grunt which could have been his way of thanking Ralph for the information, or it could have been a sign of indifference respecting the Brewsters.

When they were seen, someone raised a rifle and waved with it. One of the men trudging along waved back.

The buildings sat upon a height of the curving large land-swell, prominent because there was nothing else in the immediate vicinity. There were several large old trees both in front and in the back. The outbuildings, also of red-brick except for one which was of wood, were neat. If any weeds or underbrush ever had the temerity to appear a sharp hoe in the powerful hands of men accustomed to waging life-long war against such interlopers had cut them down, for although there was a handsome expanse of grass both front and rear, with some rose trees and other cultivated plants, everything fitted an obvious growth-pattern.

A medium-sized shaggy dog came to the verge of the soggy field to bark a welcome to the newcomers, wagging his tail in mild excitement. He had no idea that all this unexpected company wasn't arriving for something special, perhaps like a cook-out, but he thought perhaps this must be so and was delighted to see the strangers.

Collier pressed steadily ahead of the others putting Mackenzie McAuliffe in mind of another kind of dog — a hunting hound. He even smiled over the private thought. No one else smiled and when the group reached solid ground and paused to kick off the mud for the last time, Brewster freed himself from Collier and came over to offer a big hand to Ralph Fielding.

He was a large, heavy, powerful man with craggy features and a tough look in his eyes even when he smiled. Ralph introduced him to Mackenzie, then he asked about the fugitive. Brewster turned and pointed with a strong arm towards the wood outbuilding.

* * *

'He's in there. Shep raised Cain a couple of hours ago. We've been having trouble with varmints in the henhouse so my boys and I grabbed rifles and came outside. We saw him and he saw us. He ran around the side of the house. We went after him with Shep barking his fool head off.' Brewster dropped his arm and smiled. 'If he knew how surprised we were maybe he'd have kept on running out across the fields. We wouldn't have shot at him. But he ducked into the woodshed and about that time we got a telephone call from the State Police down at Brentsboro warning us to keep an eye peeled for an armed stranger. Glad they told us he was armed. We were going to flush him out. Then we saw these other fellers coming across the field. After that we just took up positions with our guns and waited.'

The policemen were milling around over nearer the house listening to Lieutenant Collier. Over there, no one smiled or spoke lightly.

Brewster's sons were identifiable by their dry feet and their bare heads. Also, they were duplicates of their father, large, heavily muscled men who would, in time look even more like the older man.

Mackenzie lit a cigarette and watched while Collier deployed his men around the shed. If the fugitive was really in there he didn't stand the chance of a snowball in hell. Even if he could break away, the countryside in all directions consisted of those open, soggy fields. There was no place to hide and he couldn't run because the mud would slow him to a fast walk.

Collier knew this end of his business very well. He was unhurried and efficient. After making certain his men were in the best positions to command a view of the shed while at the same time being protected as much as possible by the other, sturdier buildings, he went over near the rear wall of the main house and studied the shed. When he looked around and saw one of Brewster's sons he asked in a purposefully loud voice if there was any way out except by that front door. The younger Brewster confirmed that there was not.

Collier then waited a moment before calling out. For that little length of time there wasn't a sound. The sun was making steam rise from the fields. Its brightness in the clean, crisp morning air, was undiluted and brilliant. Every detail of that wooden building stood out, even to the weathered grain of each board. The door was fast closed but there were any number of cracks along the front wall the imprisoned man could peek through. If he was in there he must have watched the reinforcement of the original group that had trapped him with a sinking heart.

Of course he was armed, but attempting to shoot his way past nearly twenty other armed men must have seemed as futile, and as likely to end in death, to him, as it seemed to Ralph and Mackenzie, who were standing well to one side making no attempt to participate.

Collier called out, saying the usual things, which, trite though they might have sounded, were none the less very appropriate and very serious.

'You are completely cut off in there, mister. There isn't a chance in a hundred of you coming through this alive if you make a fight of it.'

Collier waited, head slightly cocked as though he wished to be certain of hearing correctly anything that might be said from inside the shed. Nothing was said, the silence closed down and mingled with the rising warmth. Collier called forward again.

'We'll come in there if we have to, mister, but the chances are you won't walk out if we do that. Now I'm suggesting for your own sake that you throw out your weapon and come out.'

Perhaps surprisingly, perhaps not so surprisingly, all things considered, the man in the shed answered Collier.

'I need guarantees,' he said, in a voice that did not quaver at all, but rather was strong and calm.

Collier said, instantly, 'Toss out your weapon and you'll be perfectly safe. Under arrest, naturally, but perfectly safe.'

The door opened a crack and with every eye riveted on that opening, a black automatic pistol sailed out and landed on the hot, wet grass. The weapon glistened ominously.

The man in the shed said, 'Satisfied?'

Collier answered calmly. 'Quite. Now walk out of there. Slowly, without making any quick moves. Walk towards the house and keep both your hands in plain sight.'

The door opened wider. A little interval of hushed, tense silence ensued, then a man strolled forth and blinked in the dazzling sunlight.

No one knew him. Ralph, half expecting to recognise the stranger for some indefinable reason, was disappointed. He'd never seen the man before. Mackenzie asked and Ralph shook his head.

'Complete stranger, Mackenzie.'

Collier said, 'Walk ahead, mister, towards my voice. That's fine. Keep both hands in the clear.'

The farm dog was the only one who moved as the stranger obeyed Collier. Shep strolled over, tail wagging, to sniff at the stranger's footprints in the grass.

Collier told the man when to stop. He then called in the others and while Collier kept the man covered, he directed Deputy Ames to search the prisoner.

Finally, Ralph and Mackenzie came

closer. The stranger, a somewhat stringy, lean and saturnine man, turned to look at Ralph. He seemed to either know who Ralph was or suspect, for he kept studying Ralph even when Lieutenant Collier crisply spoke again.

'Your name, mister, and your story. Speak up.'

The prisoner looked back at Collier. If the man felt any trepidation it was impossible to see signs of it in his thin face.

'Name's Aspinelli. Hugo Aspinelli. I was just poaching a little when all you fellers surrounded me.'

The man smiled bitterly straight at Collier. He was no novice and had just made that fact known. Collier put up his pistol and glared.

'You were poaching,' he said. 'What kind of game were you poaching, four-legged or two-legged? Why did you kill Mister Fielding last night?'

The sneering eyes widened in mock surprise. 'Mister who? What are you talking about?'

Collier reddened. 'Bordhese is dead, or

did you know that? And what was your personal connection with the Fieldings?'

Aspinelli raised an eyebrow and glanced again at Ralph. 'Who are the Fieldings?' he asked, mocking Collier.

Mackenzie McAuliffe said, 'Why don't you make it easy on yourself? You were over there near the Fielding house last night.'

'Prove it,' snarled the captive.

McAuliffe nodded. 'Sure. I'll swear to it in court.'

'You didn't see me!'

'I saw you. Once last night, again this morning while you were standing just in front of some trees to the west of the house waiting for someone — or for *something*, another signal-light or something like that. You bet I saw you.'

Aspinelli let his glare linger a moment longer on McAuliffe, then turned back to face Lieutenant Collier.

'Take me in if you're going to,' he snarled. 'Get me away from this bunch of fools.'

Collier said he would oblige as soon as someone brought up a car, which had been radioed for, but in the meantime he'd like to know why Hugh Fielding had been murdered.

Aspinelli's sneer curved into a cruel smile. 'I bet you would at that, but I can't help you. I never seen Hugh Fielding in my life. I can swear to that on a stack of Bibles.'

'Bordhese,' said Ralph. 'Where did he know my father?'

Aspinelli shrugged. 'As far as I know, feller, he didn't know him.'

'Then why did he shoot him?'

Aspinelli said, 'Did he? How unfortunate.'

Ralph's shoulders rolled up. For a second it looked as though he might attack Aspinelli. Collier, seeing this, stepped half between them. Then Ralph loosened and the moment passed.

Aspinelli then said, 'Look, I was out hunting with Frank Bordhese and this storm come up. We got lost out here. We're city boys so we didn't know where we were. Then we saw that big stone house over there and was going to approach it asking for shelter, when all at once three guys started shooting at us.'

Aspinelli didn't tell his story as though he expected anyone to actually believe it, he told it the way a man would recite something he was trying to commit to memory so that each time he was asked a pertinent question he could repeat this tale. Ridiculous as the story was not one of the listening bystanders really believed it would be broken even in court. And they also knew something else: Many, many men just as deadly and just as guilty as Aspinelli, had been freed by jurymen who *did* believe such a story.

Lieutenant Collier and the other peace officers were concerned with Aspinelli as a prisoner. Ralph and Mackenzie were interested in Aspinelli as a *man*; as an individual with a secret they wanted very much to share.

What the law did with Aspinelli was of secondary importance; what the men from Masters Manor had to know what *why* Hugh Fielding had been murdered, and *why* that frightful all-night siege had been undertaken.

But the police car came whipping up the farm road before any answers were given, Collier loaded his captive in and with a curt order for the others to disband, Collier was swiftly driven off in the direction of Brentsboro, in the company of his sneering prisoner.

21

A Slender Thread

Ralph told Mackenzie that tired and dirty or not, if he'd had his car handy he'd have followed Collier to Brentsboro to interrogate the prisoner.

Instead, however, they were returned to Masters Manor in one of the other cars, to discover that everyone there already knew of the capture, thanks to the good offices of Police Lieutenant Peter Collier.

Ralph's reaction was to tell Mackenzie it was entirely out of character for Collier to be so concerned over the desire of the people at Masters Manor to know this. Mackenzie said he would suspect Lieutenant Collier of having an ulterior motive.

Betty, the Olmsteads, Emilio Calderon, wanted to hear each detail of the capture. Sadly, neither Ralph nor Mackenzie could give them any blow-by-blow saga of clever tracking, wily manoeuvres that had resulted in the cornering of the assassin, then of a heroic gunfight in which right triumphed and wrong went down to its deserved and bitter defeat.

In fact, when they finished telling how Aspinelli got himself caught in a woodshed, and how he meekly surrendered, Frank Olmstead, evidently feeling better than he'd been feeling, said through a cloud of cigar smoke, 'Isn't that a hell of a note,' and as inelegant as this statement may have been, none could deny how very appropriate it was.

In the absence of Ralph and Mackenzie, Frank Olmstead had not been idle. Betty told the two younger men that Olmstead had called his attorney, had called the Brentsboro office of the State Police to raise Cain over his impounded helicopter, and had also called someone down in New York aside from his attornies, presumably his office, although he'd closed the study door when he'd made that call.

Ralph went upstairs to bath and

change. Afterwards, alone, he went out to the back where the yardman, with a most lugubrious expression, showed him where that uprooted tree had left a hole in the turf something like four feet deep and almost fifteen feet across. Also, there was a noticeable crack in the house's rear stone wall where the falling tree had struck.

Ralph gave the yardman instructions to cut up the tree for firewood and to have the hole filled in when the ground was firm enough to support the weight of dumptrucks. As for the wall of Masters Manor, he'd see to that himself, in good time.

He returned to the study by way of the sunroom and met Emilio standing near the study window, hands behind his back looking out where sunshine was working diligently at healing many of the wounds caused by that nocturnal cloudburst. Emilio turned, smiling ruefully. 'What do we know?' he asked. 'Except that the police now have the other man, what do we know?' He didn't permit Ralph to answer but turned and gestured out where the police helicopter had been. It was gone. 'Two men came in a car, one flew it away. Neither of them came to the house. If they had perhaps we'd have known something.'

Ralph sympathised with the Central American's mood. Most certainly everyone in the house who had lived through that incredible night wished to know — and *deserved* to know — what it had all been about.

Ralph reached for the telephone. By now Lieutenant Collier, or someone down at Brentsboro who had charge of interrogating prisoners — should have got something out of Aspinelli. He dialled, had no difficulty at all reaching the correct telephone, but he didn't get Collier. Another police officer said that Lieutenant Collier was out and probably wouldn't be back until mid-afternoon or perhaps even later. Ralph asked about Aspinelli. The policeman's answer was predictable: He could not volunteer any information about prisoners.

'Just tell me one thing,' persisted young Fielding. Did someone interrogate him?'

'Oh yes,' replied the officer. 'He was interrogated. That's usually mandatory before a person is booked into gaol.'

'And did he talk at all? I mean, at the Brewster farm all he did was sneer and act clever.'

The policeman's reply was faintly brusque. 'He talked, Mister Fielding, but any other information will have to come from Lieutenant Collier himself. Goodbye.'

What Emilio hadn't figured out for himself, from his one-sided version of this conversation, Ralph explained to him. Emilio was hopeful but before he could do more than express his faith in the methods of Lieutenant Collier, Mary-Katherine Olmstead came into the study from the living-room, gazed at the two men, then smiled and said in her most sultry tone of voice she hadn't meant to intrude upon so handsome a pair of conspirators.

Emilio, always gallant, explained that they'd been trying to elicit information from the police about the prisoner but without very much luck. He then sought to get the conversation upon more pleasant grounds by saying that as soon as someone would drive him down to retrieve his Jaguar, where Ralph had abandoned it long before, he would be delighted to drive Mary-Katherine and her husband back to New York City.

The woman smiled softly upon Emilio. She was stone-sober. She was also dressed differently than when Ralph and Mackenzie had gone away with Lieutenant Collier shortly after daybreak. She looked clean and rested and quite fit. Her husband, she said, was upstairs packing their things; she thought he might have made arrangements for a car-hire outfit to come and get them. But if he hadn't done this, she told Emilio with one of her sexiest looks, she would love to ride all the way down to New York with Calderon.

Ralph, watching the woman turn on her charm, also saw how Calderon wilted under it. Any other time he might have felt amused; now he only felt a little sorry for the Latin American's susceptibility, and more than just a little contempt for the woman's willingness to be this brazen before a third person. It occurred to Ralph that Olmstead's eagle-eyed watchfulness of his wife was well deserved.

Emilio left the study with Mary-Katherine, which pleased Ralph who'd come in there originally to make a private telephone call, and had been prevented from making it by Calderon's unexpected presence. He let the man and woman get well across the living-room towards the bar before stepping over to gently close the study door, then go back and telephone his father's office in the city.

There, he picked up a very interesting scrap of information. His father, prior to leaving the office on Friday, had telephoned a private detective agency. Until one of the gentlemen from that company had showed up earlier this same day with a confidential envelope for Hugh Fielding, his administrative assistant at the ad agency had had no idea any such arrangement had been entered into. Hugh Fielding had not mentioned it, although he normally told his assistant everything he did. The assistant's explanation was plausible, though.

'It probably had nothing whatever to do with the agency, and of course if this were the case, why then he'd have no reason to confide in me.'

Whether the man was piqued or not was not at the moment of much interest to Ralph. He said, 'What's in the envelope?'

The answer was faintly stiff. 'I haven't opened it. It was handed to me to be given to your father in confidence.'

'Do you have it handy?' asked Ralph, and upon being informed that in fact the assistant had it before him on his desk, Ralph said, 'Open it, read the contents to me.'

The man hesitated, inhibited by years of obedience to his employer. Ralph's exasperation made him repeat the order. 'Open it! My father is dead — murdered — and I want to know if there's anything in that envelope that might have a bearing upon that fact!'

The assistant opened the letter and read what was inside in a quiet voice. 'The heading directs your father's attention to the fact, Mister Fielding, that a bill is also enclosed for the following information, and I quote: 'Frank Swanson Olmstead is interested in the sea-frontage development in Italy precisely as he has told you. The title to that land is clear and unencumbered, also as he told you, so at least in this respect Olmstead did not misrepresent anything. However, according to the Italian police there has been some question about Olmstead's connection with local smugglers who have used that area for a good many years. The police think Olmstead was either bought off or warned off, or perhaps joined with the smugglers, whose primary import is drugs which they receive from Dutch ships returning from the Far East. This is the major seat of the Italian drug-smuggling business, and the police say they have been working in conjunction with other European police for over a year now to expose the entire affair, because it is through this means that Europe's major drug markets are supplied. The Italian police estimate the business may be worth as much as ten million U.S. dollars annually.' ' For a moment the droning voice was silent, then it said, 'Ralph, obviously, your father was having second thoughts about Olmstead, and his proposal that he and your father form a partnership.'

Ralph, standing beside his father's desk until now, sat down. At the other end of the line the voice said, 'Are you still there, Ralph?' The answer was quietly given. 'Yes, I'm still here. Keep that information locked up and don't mention any of this to anyone.' Ralph rang off, fished for a cigarette, lit it and swivelled in the deskchair to gaze soberly out the window behind the desk where a beautiful afternoon was just beginning to break.

He saw the dark unmarked sedan suddenly and quietly appear in the drive out yonder, watched Lieutenant Collier alight and start for the house, and jack-knifed to his feet to head off the policeman at the front doorway.

Collier looked up when Ralph appeared. He neither nodded nor spoke, at least not for a moment, and Ralph meanwhile stepped clear of the house out into that hot sunlight with its steamy humidity, took Collier's arm and turned the policeman back towards the car Collier had just abandoned.

Oddly, Collier did not resist, although, when Ralph released his arm and leaned upon the bonnet to speak, Collier said, 'I take it you've stumbled on to something you'd prefer the others didn't hear.'

Ralph studied Collier's craggy, tough features a moment, then said, 'What did Aspinelli tell you, Lieutenant?'

'That's privileged information, Mister Fielding.'

Ralph's mouth flattened a little. 'I'm sure it is. But suppose I told you one of us who spent the night here is suspected by the European police of having a hand in a ten-million-dollar-per-year dope smuggling enterprise?'

Collier simply said, 'I wouldn't be at all surprised, Mister Fielding. And supposing I were to tell you that Hugo Aspinelli has a police record as long as your arm ranging from aggravated assault as a youngster, to killing for hire now? Eighteen arraignments and four convictions. Unfortunately, the convictions were never for the right crimes, otherwise of course he wouldn't have been free, would he have?'

'Is that the privileged information?' asked Ralph.

Collier smiled crookedly. 'Part of it. Enough, I trust, to inspire you to volunteer what you know.'

Ralph explained about the confidential information bought by his father. Collier was interested. He lit a cigarette, let it droop from his lips and gave the back of his hands his undivided attention for a silent moment. Then he said, 'Frankly, Aspinelli did not implicate anyone out here. He has perfected that silly story of being out hunting — in a raging storm, mind, and with a pistol instead of a rifle — and refuses to budge from it. Of course he's thinking ahead to a trial. But he did say one thing that interested me, so I went over to the coroner's office this morning. He said his friend Bordhese was not an American citizen.'

'Bordhese, as you doubtless saw, was also the name of that ship's captain who traded along the coastal ports of Italy.'

'Yes, of course, and now, with what you've turned up, we can guess what he traded in, and perhaps we can also surmise that is what occasioned his trouble — he either tried to hold out some of a dope shipment, or someone hi-jacked him for it. But that's not very important, except for one thing. The so-called dead man, Michael King — more properly Franklin Delano Bordhese — was the younger brother of that ship's captain. I verified that easily enough through the New York Police Department.' Collier glanced towards the front of the house. 'Is Olmstead still in there?'

'Yes.'

'Suppose you lend me a hand, then, Mister Fielding. I'll talk to him in the study and if you'll keep the others away, I'm sure we'll progress one step closer to the solution to our riddle.'

Collier smiled at Ralph. This time it was a genuine smile, although, granting that he'd decided to accept Ralph Fielding as a temporary aide, the smile still was not entirely frank nor open.

Ralph wasn't concerned; he simply wanted to meet the person who was responsible for the killer of his father showing up last night. He nodded and led the way back into the house.

22

Surprise and Confrontation!

They hit a snag straight away. Olmstead told Lieutenant Collier he would not enter the study with him, and he would not answer any questions at all, upon the advice of his lawyer down in New York City.

Collier had an alternative, of course; he could arrest Frank Olmstead on suspicion of complicity, but that wasn't the best thing to arrest a wealthy and belligerent person for.

Collier sourly stood in the centre of the living-room gazing stonily at Frank Olmstead. The others were all there, and they also had their luggage standing over beside the front door. Mackenzie said they'd been informed by the Department of Public Works down at Brentsboro there would be an adequate temporary bridge spanning the subsiding creek by four in the afternoon.

He and Emilio and Frank Olmstead had spent the last hour or so locating their ignition failures and making the cars operable again. There was nothing left to detain any of them, unless of course that temporary bridge wasn't completed as promised, by four o'clock, or unless Lieutenant Collier officially detained them. The latter, while a possibility, wasn't actually causing much consternation. None of these people were wholly ignorant of their rights under the law, and as far as Collier was concerned, if he *did* detain them, he'd want to be very certain he was within his authority. Frank Olmstead, for example, was the type of person to spend a fortune trying to get Collier's badge.

Collier knew it. He stood gazing upon Olmstead as though he'd have enjoyed striking the larger man. And after a bit he said, 'Mister Olmstead, what prompted Bordhese to come out here? Had Fielding already decided not to form a partnership with you, and you wanted to either frighten him into reconsidering, or wished to have revenge for his disappointing you?'

'What in the holy hell are you talking about?' exclaimed Olmstead. 'Lieutenant, you're even wilder than I thought you were. Hugh and I were going to finalise our partnership arrangement over the weekend. Why would I want revenge for that?'

'He wasn't going to form a partnership with you,' said Collier, and jerked his head. 'Ask Ralph.'

The look on Olmstead's face was too genuine to be false when he looked at young Fielding. His eyes were totally puzzled. 'What's this ridiculous policeman talking about?' he demanded of Ralph. 'Of course we were going to form a partnership. Why else would he invite me out here — why else would I have come?'

Ralph knew his father well. He believed at least part of what had just been said. Unless his father had really intended to discuss business with Olmstead he never would have invited the man to Masters Manor. Ralph saw the way Olmstead was looking at him and suddenly remembered something. He knew if he accused Olmstead of anything the man would ringingly deny it, so he said, 'I would be inclined to believe what you say, Mister Olmstead, except for one thing. I saw you break the telephone line in the study with your heel.'

It was not the truth but the silence that descended among them all seemed to give that prevarication solid substance. Calderon nodded softly from his chair, probably also recalling that Olmstead had been in the study when the telephone went dead for the second time, but the nod appeared as support for the lie.

Olmstead paled. 'It was an accident,' he said. Obviously the man had prepared this alibi well in advance. 'Afterwards I knew how it would look if I mentioned stepping on the damned thing, so I said nothing.' He shrugged, looked around, began to get a little colour back in his cheeks and said, 'But I tell you absolutely — I had nothing whatever to do with the killing of Hugh Fielding. Good God; why would I do that? And if I wanted it done, would I be right here, liable to be suspected myself?'

'Now,' said Ralph, 'tell us that you didn't know the man we killed — Bordhese?'

'Oh hell,' snorted Olmstead. 'Of course I knew him. Well, not personally, you see, but I knew his brother in Italy. What of it?'

Collier dropped a real bombshell. He said, 'Mister Olmstead, it was a close call, wasn't it? Bordhese and Aspinelli didn't come here to kill Hugh Fielding at all. *They came here to kill you*!'

Even Ralph was stiffened into stunned silence by that statement. So was everyone else. They all looked at Lieutenant Collier, waiting for whatever he would say next. But he simply stood over there near the fireplace, watching Frank Olmstead with his gaze bitter and bleak.

Olmstead went to a chair and dropped into it. 'You're out of your mind,' he muttered. It wasn't convincing at all. All the man's arrogance seemed to desert him. He had to cave in sometime of course, after all no one could go on indefinitely putting up a bold front.

He looked straight at Ralph. 'Believe me, I did not have anything whatever to do with your father's death.'

Collier said, 'Indirectly, Mister Olmstead, you were the *cause* of his death.'

Olmstead doggedly shook his head. 'No. I didn't want him hurt. Lord Almighty, if we'd formed that partnership, if he'd created a campaign to sell my Italian sea-frontage to the international set for villas, we'd both have made millions.'

'Maybe,' agreed Collier. 'You probably would have. But would that money be as much as you'd have made from smuggling?'

Olmstead seemed to reel in his chair as though from a solid blow but he didn't speak. Automatically, he reached inside his coat and lit up one of those inevitable cigars, but it seemed to be a defensive move, something to do to gain time by. He blew smoke, rallied a little and gazed past them all as though they hadn't been in the room, to look directly at his wife. She sat relaxed in a chair near Emilio Calderon watching him with the eyes of a tethered falcon, with the expression of a viper observing the destruction of a natural enemy.

It was Mackenzie McAuliffe who broke that silence. He said, 'By the way, if anyone is really very interested, it wasn't Olmstead who gave those signals from my room with the flashlight, last night.'

Collier and Ralph turned. The others also had their attention drawn away from the other man by this casual statement. McAuliffe and his wife were sitting on the same stained sofa where Calderon, and later, where Dubois the butler, had been lying; they were calm and poised.

'Would you care to elaborate,' asked Lieutenant Collier with exaggerated sarcasm, 'Mister McAuliffe?'

Mackenzie swung his eyes to Mary-Katherine Olmstead. 'She did the signalling.'

Mary-Katherine neither moved nor made a sound. She simply looked back at Mackenzie with that same venomous expression in her eyes she'd used towards her husband.

'Care to offer your theory on that?' asked Collier.

'No theory,' said McAuliffe. 'Pure fact. And if you want substantiation, ask her husband.'

Collier turned. 'Mister Olmstead . . . ?'

The answer from the harassed husband was predictable 'I told you, my lawyer said I was to say nothing at all until —.'

Mackenzie cut in sharply, his whole manner changing. 'Tell them why you left the kitchen, Olmstead. Not the lie you told Ralph about not wanting your wife upstairs alone. Tell them you knew she was signalling those assassins and went up there to stop her.'

Olmstead finally looked at Mackenzie. So did the others, particularly Lieutenant Collier who was suddenly quite interested, but most of all, Frank Olmstead stared with glassy eyes.

McAuliffe spoke on. 'Each time she went upstairs last night, you went up and brought her back down. My wife noticed that. A little while ago she and I sat down to compare thoughts. Then there was the obvious running feud that's been going on between you ever since you arrived here.'

'My wife drinks too much,' said Olmstead. 'I told you that. I simply wanted to stop that before she made a scene.'

Collier growled them all into silence, then said, 'Mister McAuliffe, I'd like to hear more about this signalling.'

'Every time it happened Mrs. Olmstead was upstairs. That time Ralph saw it when he was out getting wood, she was up there. *She was the only person absent from the living-room* except for her husband.'

'Then how can you be sure *he* wasn't flashing those signals, Mister McAuliffe?'

Finally, Betty McAuliffe entered the conversation.

'Lieutenant,' she said softly, 'you read those two letters found on that dead Italian, didn't you?'

Collier bridled a little; obviously, he didn't understand Italian. 'I got the drift of them, yes. What of it?'

'One was signed 'Gina' and it was from a woman in New York City. She evidently was in love with this man who used the name of King, perhaps the name of Reino as well, but whose actual name was Bordhese.'

'Go on,' said Collier.

Betty glanced swiftly at her husband as though for moral support. He smiled so she turned back towards Collier and said, 'Lieutenant, my husband and I had the room next to the Olmsteads last night. We didn't hear what was happening downstairs until the gunshot sounded, but moments before, as though someone had looked at a clock, Mrs. Olmstead told her husband to go downstairs and bring up her cigarettes which she'd left on the bar. He refused, telling her to go to sleep. They had a fierce argument which was interrupted by that gunshot. After that there was absolute silence until we heard Ralph screaming for help for his father.'

Collier frowned. 'Would you mind getting to the point, Mrs. McAuliffe?'

'The point, Lieutenant, is that the assassin who came to the door, did so at a pre-arranged time, where he was to find Frank Olmstead prowling in the living-room, and shoot him.

'What really happened is that Hugh Fielding, for some reason we'll never know — perhaps he was disturbed by the storm, perhaps he was too restless to sleep — went downstairs, and Frank Olmstead refused to go as his wife wished him to do, with the result that in the poor light, Hugh Fielding was shot to death in error.'

Collier stood staring at Betty McAuliffe. Ralph also stared at her. Then those two looked at one another. They had already decided Ralph's father had been killed by mistake. Collier raised his brows in Mary-Katherine's direction. She spat at him. 'Completely asinine. Absolutely without a shred of truth to it.'

Then they all saw the white look on her husband's face as he sat like stone looking at Mary-Katherine. He made a little sound in his throat, half moan, half gasp.

He said, 'It is the truth.'

Collier moved lightly as Mary-Katherine casually reached for her large purse. He struck the thing, knocking it to the floor.

Its contents spilled — including a little flashlight like the one taken from the dead assassin, and a small, ugly little Baretta automatic pistol. Collier scooped up the pistol first, then the flashlight. He turned, examining those things, and said, 'Mister Olmstead . . . ?'

The older man leaned forward as though suddenly afflicted with stomach pains. 'It is the truth,' he said. 'She met Bordhese in Italy last summer. I knew what was going on, so I brought her home. He followed. I knew that too, but I kept her close to me. Well, I knew she hated my guts, but not murder. I didn't think she'd do that.'

'You knew Bordhese and Aspinelli were out there last night?' asked Ralph Fielding.

'Not until I caught her signalling. Then I wrung it out of her.'

'Didn't you suspect they were here to kill you?'

'No, I thought they were here to take her away.'

Lieutenant Collier said, 'Mister Olmstead — about that smuggling . . . ?'

'She and the Bordheses. I knew that too. But I had no part of it.'

'The Italian police thought you had a hand in it,' said Collier quietly.

'No. That was nothing I cared to become involved in.'

Mackenzie had a question. 'Why was Calderon returned to the house after being struck over the head, and who unlocked that door in the cellar?'

Olmstead said bitterly, 'Ask *her*!'

Mary-Katherine spat a fierce curse at her husband. 'I should have shot you myself, last night.' She saw Collier watching her and defiantly said, 'I unlocked the damned door. The reason they brought Calderon inside was to scare the others into trying to get away — to make them think there were killers inside the house. They waited by the cars to get Frank when we all ran out. Only it didn't work that way.'

Emilio Calderon, who had fallen victim to Mary-Katherine's charm, said in a low, prayerful voice. '*Madre de Dios!*' and turned his head away.

Betty asked Olmstead's wife a question.

'Mary-Katherine, were you the 'Gina' in that letter?'

Mrs. Olmstead shrugged. 'That's what *he* called me in Italy.' She sneered at her husband. '*He* was my lover, not Frank, who was a pig and always has been one.'

Lieutenant Collier blew out a big breath, turned and said, 'Mister Olmstead, I'll ask you to come along voluntarily, please. Your wife is under arrest for complicity in the murder of Hugh Fielding.'

Olmstead got heavily to his feet. Ralph Fielding, Mackenzie McAuliffe, all the others in fact, felt pity for Olmstead, the man none of them had ever liked.

Collier said, 'It's slightly past four o'clock. If the rest of you would like to leave now, I won't detain you.'

Ralph watched Collier take the Olmsteads across the room and out of the front door. Then he turned and looked at the others. No one said anything.

It was over, a nightmare lifetime compressed into something like eighteen hours.

Outside the afternoon sun was soft and beckoning, and beyond the rural New England countryside was the other world, the one they all belonged to. They were glad to be able to return to it.

THE END

Other titles in the Linford Mystery Library

A LANCE FOR THE DEVIL
Robert Charles

The funeral service of Pope Paul VI was to be held in the great plaza before St. Peter's Cathedral in Rome, and was to be the scene of the most monstrous mass assassination of political leaders the world had ever known. Only Counter-Terror could prevent it.

IN THAT RICH EARTH
Alan Sewart

How long does it take for a human body to decay until only the bones remain? When Detective Sergeant Harry Chamberlane received news of a body, he raised exactly that question. But whose was the body? Who was to blame for the death and in what circumstances?

MURDER AS USUAL
Hugh Pentecost

A psychotic girl shot and killed Mac Crenshaw, who had come to the New England town with the advance party for Senator Farraday. Private detective David Cotter agreed that the girl was probably just a pawn in a complex game — but who had sent her on the assignment?

THE MARGIN
Ian Stuart

It is rumoured that Walkers Brewery has been selling arms to the South African army, and Graham Lorimer is asked to investigate. He meets the beautiful Shelley van Rynveld, who is dedicated to ending apartheid. When a Walkers employee is killed in a hit-and-run accident, his wife tells Graham that he's been seeing Shelly van Rynveld . . .

TOO LATE FOR THE FUNERAL
Roger Ormerod

Carol Turner, seventeen, and a mystery, is very close to a murder, and she has in her possession a weapon that could prove a number of things. But it is Elsa Mallin who suffers most before the truth of Carol Turner releases her.

NIGHT OF THE FAIR
Jay Baker

The gun was the last of the things for which Harry Judd had fought and now it was in the hands of his worst enemy, aimed at the boy he had tried to help. This was the night in which the past had to be faced again and finally understood.